YOU CAN'T
KISS IT BETTER

Also by Diana Hendry in Red Fox

Harvey Angell
Harvey Angell and the Ghost Child
Harvey Angell Beats Time

The Awesome Bird

YOU CAN'T
KISS IT BETTER
DIANA HENDRY

Red Fox

A RED FOX BOOK: 0 099403471

First published in Great Britain by Red Fox
an imprint of Random House Children's Books

Red Fox edition published 2003

1 3 5 7 9 10 8 6 4 2

Papers used by Random House Children's Books are natural,
recyclable products made from wood grown in sustainable forests.
The manufacturing processes conform to the environmental
regulations of the country of origin

Set in Linotype Sabon
Red Fox Books are published by Random House Children's Books,
61-63 Uxbridge Road, London W5 5SA,

a division of The Random House Group Ltd,
in Australia by Random House Australia (Pty) Ltd,
20 Alfred Street, Milsons Point, Sydney, NSW 2061, Australia,
in New Zealand by Random House New Zealand Ltd,
18 Poland Road, Glenfield, Auckland 10, New Zealand,
and in South Africa by Random House (Pty) Ltd,
Endulini, 5A Jubilee Road. Parktown 2193, South Africa

THE RANDOM HOUSE GROUP Limited Reg. No. 954009
www.kidsatrandomhouse.co.uk

A CIP catalogue record for this book is available from
the British Library.

Printed and bound in Great Britain by
Bookmarque Ltd, Croydon, Surrey

FOR DELIA

− BEST OF EDITORS, BEST OF FRIENDS −

WITH LOVE

Acknowledgements

I would like to thank the following people who helped me write this book – Ian Millar, Social Work Consultant with British Agencies for Adoption and Fostering (Scottish Centre) and Alan Jackson, Service Manager Children and Families, Social Work Department, City of Edinburgh Council, for information on fostering and adoption. Edith Wellwood for her very careful and thoughtful reading of the manuscript – not once, but twice! Alison Smith for talks about and walks along the river. P. C. Gordon McBain of Lothian and Borders Police Force for advice and information. My daughter, Kate, most dear and gentle critic.

The publishers gratefully acknowledge permission to reprint lines from Ted Hughes' 'The River in March' from his collection *Season Songs*, © Ted Hughes 1985, published by Faber and Faber Ltd; and for verses from 'Look At The Children' by W. S. Graham, copyright the Estate of W. S. Graham.

Look at the children of the world
Looking out at us to say hello
All from their lonely photographs.

What's to be done? What's to be done?
The hungry dogs are come to town.
Where have your father and mother gone?

Look at the children of the world
Breaking our hearts but not enough
While we eat our money up.

from: *Look At The Children* by W. S. Graham

THE RIVER COULD TELL THIS STORY. The river starts high in the Pentland Hills then nips and tucks its way through the outlying villages until it enters the heart of the city. Then off it goes, throwing itself over the weir in a roaring sheen of molten silver, plummeting down the gorge, hurrying under the tall grand bridge, then the little low bridge, on past cemeteries, old warehouses, tall rich houses with tumbling gardens until at last it joins its great grandparent, the sea.

The river could tell stories that are centuries old. It could tell of the millers and tanners, the snuff- and papermakers who once worked by and with the river. It could tell of badgers, stoats and foxes; swans, ducks, bats and owls. Generations of bluebells, snowdrops, brambles and nettles are remembered by the river as are the children. Children who swam and fished and dreamt and wished here – children like Anna, Raymond and Sam who live with Megan in her rambling house high above the river.

Megan's house isn't one of the rich ones, though once upon a time it might have been. Megan's house needs just about everything doing to it, from a new roof to windows that close properly and heating that does more than groan and gurgle. Anna, Raymond and Sam aren't exactly a family. They're more what Megan calls a *jumbily*, a jumble of people trying to *become* a family.

For those like Megan and her jumbily, the river's not an easy companion. It's moody. There are days when it's slow and dreamy. Days when the wind's up and the water rises and the river becomes all busy and cheerful. On days like this it hurries along as if it's saying to itself 'Can't wait, can't wait! Off to sea! Off to sea!', all self-important and pleased with itself. For weeks on end the river can seem quiet and playful and you could convince yourself that it's a nice, kindly creature. That's when it turns nasty. That's when it's like someone in prison who's mad to get out. That's when it hurls itself over the weir as if it's hell bent on smashing everything and everyone in its way. It's all roar and rush and hullabaloo and you'd best keep out of its way.

The moods of the river are like the moods in Megan's house. You might wonder if the weather affected people the way it affected the river so that when the river's angry, someone in the house is angry too. Maybe Raymond. Or maybe Anna. Or Sam. Megan thinks this is nonsense.

There's only one person who knows the true secrets of the river and that's the River Woman. But the River Woman won't tell, won't talk. That's why it's Anna who begins this story.

Chapter One

THIS IS MY FOURTH foster home. 21 Teviotdale Place, EH10 4HY. You get to remember addresses really quickly when you move around. My social worker, Clara, says I ought to write a Life Story Book. They like to get kids doing things like that so that when you go to your next place, they know something about you. Who your tummy-mummy was. What vaccinations you've had. How you've been doing at school. Stuff like that.

Clara says, 'It's nice to have a records of the past, Anna. You could do drawings. Put some pictures in.'

But I don't want to do any of that. I want to write my *own* book with my *own* thoughts in it. I'm not too keen on facts. Facts don't tell you that much about a person, do they? I mean things like, 'I was born on April 5, 1990 at Victoria Infirmary. Weight 6 lbs 4 oz.' What does that tell you? That I was a skinny baby and that I'm twelve. That's what. It doesn't tell you anything about me, *now*.

I've been here three months. There's just me and Raymond. Raymond's ten and doesn't speak. It's not that he *can't* speak. It's just that he *won't* speak. Or only when he must. He's got this tight little closed-up face. He can't bear anyone touching him either. Not that I try. But Megan does. Megan's our foster mum. She's keen on hugs. The only thing Raymond cares about is Toby. Toby's the dog. He's got black and white patches like a cow and a tail like a question mark. He belongs to Megan really but he's taken to Raymond and Raymond's taken to Toby. Big time!

Raymond's in long-term foster care. There's three kinds of foster care – short-term, long-term and permanent. Oh and emergency. I'm shortish. I expect I'll be going home any day now. My mum's a famous actress. You've probably seen her on TV. I shall be one too, one day. Or maybe a famous author. I haven't decided yet.

This place is better than the last one. The foster parents were Mr and Mrs Thomas. He worked with computers and she was a teacher. They said they couldn't cope with me because I was always making up stories and disturbing the other children with them. I was a 'disruption'. Major. Some of the stories I made up on Mr Thomas's computer. He didn't like that at all. Said I'd destroyed some records he badly needed. Megan doesn't have a computer. It's a shame. I could write this book much better if I had a nice little laptop or something. Megan doesn't have a husband either. Well, I think she had one once, but he's gone. 'Vanished off the face of the earth,' Megan said. Though he can't have done, can he? Unless he's on another planet. Which is possible, I suppose. Maybe one night he'll come back on a space shuttle or something. But I hope not.

Anyway, what Clara (my social worker, remember?) said to the Thomases when I left, was, 'Anna is rather given to magical thinking.' She put her arm round me when she said it.

I don't quite know what magical thinking is, but I like the sound of it. I think I may have a talent for it. The Thomases were very factual people. I don't think Megan is like that because this house isn't all tidy like the Thomases' was. Or tried to be. It's rather a mess, in fact. Fact! Ha ha. But a comfy sort of mess. And it's right by the river. That's the best thing of all. I can look out of my bedroom window and see the river. And I can hear it at night. Burbling along. Sometimes slow, sometimes fast.

I like the river because when I was at the Thomases' I read this book – well, not *all* of it, called *The Wind in the Willows*. Mrs Thomas (I always called her that) had these really old books that she said had belonged to her little girl. Most of them were really dull. Anyway, *The Wind in the Willows* was about these animals that live by the river. They can all talk, so I reckon the author was quite good at magical thinking, too. What really got me was that right at the beginning it talks about spring arriving with a 'spirit of divine discontent and longing'. I think that's what I've got. Divine discontent and longing. Course I've got *ordinary* discontent, too. Like being fed up about moving from house to house. And ordinary longings, too. Like for a lap top and for that T-shirt I saw in *Kookai* last Saturday.

I told Mrs Thomas I had divine discontent one night when she was going on at me about tidying up my bedroom and not deliberately tearing my clothes. (I've got a bit of a habit about that. It's just when I'm anxious.)

'I've got divine discontent,' I said and Mrs Thomas said, 'Anna, *nobody* has divine discontent these days.'

That's what she thinks. I don't suppose she's ever read *The Wind in the Willows*, or if she has, she's forgotten. Anyway, you know if you've got it, divine discontent and longing that is, because you feel it in your stomach. It's a kind of empty feeling as if you really badly, badly want something only you don't know what it is. Maybe I'll find out. Maybe the River Woman will tell me.

I only saw the River Woman last week. She's very, very old. About two hundred and fifty I'd guess. Old enough to know *everything*. She wades about the river in these old wellies and sometimes she has a bonfire on the banks. I said 'hello' to her the other day but she just stared at me and grunted. She's got these piercing blue eyes. I didn't tell Megan about her because Megan would be sure to make up another House Rule about not talking to strange old women who make bonfires.

Every house I've been in has had different House Rules. You'd think the government would make a list so we could all have the same ones. I mean why is it that in one house they want you to put all your dirty washing in a basket and in another house you have to bring it down and put it in the machine? And in some houses there's actually no television until five o'clock and in others it's on first thing in the morning. And you're expected to know all this as soon as you walk in the door. Or almost. When I have a house of my own I'm not going to have any rules at all.

The River Woman doesn't look as if she has rules. Her hair is very white with bits of sticks and leaves in it. I think she lives in a tree house. Without rules. Anyway, I'm going to find out. And I won't tell Raymond. Raymond thinks the river is *his*.

Our river's got willows, too, like the ones in the book. But no talking animals. Or none that I've met!

Chapter Two

I'VE HAD THIS HUGE ROW with Raymond and now Megan says I can either help clear up the mess or stay in my room until I calm down. So I'm staying in my room.

Actually, it was more of a fight than a row. But that's because it's very difficult to have a row with someone who *doesn't speak*. I suppose it's funny really that someone *not* speaking can make you feel so mad. Maybe it makes me mad because I like words. When I'm by myself I always have music on or the radio. Not because I'm really listening but just because I like voices. A person can feel very lonely when it's all quiet and silent.

Anyway, all I said to Raymond was, 'I suppose your mum didn't come.' We were watching TV after supper, Raymond, Toby-dog and me, and I suddenly remembered it was the first Monday of the month which is when Raymond's mum is meant to visit. Only she never does. Raymond pretends he doesn't care, but I know he does because the night before he often sleep-walks and on the day itself he can't eat his breakfast.

Raymond didn't answer of course. Just snuggled up to Toby-dog.

'Well, did she or didn't she?' I asked.

Just a grunt. I took it to mean 'no'.

'I expect she was busy with your little sister,' I said.

Well, I meant it kindly. Like a kind of excuse. But Raymond suddenly punched me really hard. And then he *did* speak.

'You *never* see your mum.'

'That's because she's on tour,' I said.

'I don't think you've even *got* a mum,' Raymond said.

I was that mad I kicked Toby-dog. Next thing I knew

13

Raymond flung himself at me. He was punching me everywhere, pulling my hair, trying to bang my head on the floor. Toby-dog was going mad, barking and running round us and I was screaming and yelling and the table got knocked over and a lamp got smashed and then Megan rushed in and pulled us apart.

It's not my mum's fault she can't come and see me. And I know with all that travelling round from theatre to theatre – often in other countries – that she doesn't have time to write. It's more my fault really. My mum being very beautiful she had all these boyfriends and I hated them. Particularly the last one, Jem. I used to wish he was dead. And the next thing was, *he was*. And my mum cried for weeks and said she couldn't cope with this any more and she'd have to take up her career again and you couldn't do that with a child in tow.

But I know she loves me. I know when she's made enough money and found us a place to live, we'll all be reunited – me, my mum and my real dad. Whoever he is. I dream about him sometimes. He's got grey hair and a nice smile and I think dreaming about him means he'll come back one day. He'll find us again.

If Raymond was someone you could have a conversation with, I'd tell him all this. But you can't have a conversation with someone who won't speak. It gets to be like talking to yourself.

I don't tell them at school about my mum being a famous actress because I don't think they'd believe me. You get a lot of grief if you're a 'looked after child'.

'What you done?' Gemma Ford asked me once. 'Rob a bank?' Or sometimes it's 'Are your parents in prison?' Or 'Nobody want you then?'

I tell them I was abandoned. 'Abandoned' is just about my favourite word. And I can picture how it might have been. I'd be a tiny little thing all wrapped up in snowy blankets and left in a cardboard box on someone's doorstep. Maybe a stately home kind of doorstep. Or a castle. Though I'm not sure castles have doorsteps.

Anyway my tummy-mummy would leave me there and she'd creep away weeping. Sometimes I can picture it so well I almost think it might have happened.

Yesterday I came back from school along the river. You go down the steps near the bridge and the Pizza place and there you are. And there's ducks and swans and loads of pigeons. And dog shit on the path but you can avoid it easy if you look where you're going.

There's a big willow tree with branches that lean right over the river and that's where the pigeons like to sit. I think they're like newspaper reporters, looking up and down the river and reporting all the news. *The Pigeon Post* ha ha. Latest! Latest! SWANS HAVE CYGNET. They have too. It's a funny little grey thing and the Swan Mum and Dad fuss over it a lot. Swan Mums and Dads stay together forever. Or so Mrs Nobes, my teacher, says.

All along the wall at the far side of the river there are holes where the pigeons live. Like apartments. Like a housing estate for pigeons. If they had numbers it would go, No. 1 Pigeon Avenue and so on.

I haven't seen any rats or moles by the river, like in the book. Though I did see a toad. My favourite character in *WITW* is Mole. I like it when Mole is out with Ratty and he smells his home and suddenly this great homesick longing comes over him and he thinks his heart will break. And he knows it's a shabby, dingy little place and not grand like Toad Hall, but it's home and he loves it. I feel like that sometimes when I think of Mum and me at home in our flat and how sometimes we'd have fish and chips for tea and eat them straight out of the paper.

But what I was getting to was that I saw the River Woman again. She was actually in the river and dragging things out of it. Branches that have broken off, old bottles, a really heavy gas canister, an odd shoe, a bucket without a handle, an old car tyre. I could hear her talking to herself so I stopped to listen. 'Cleaning and burning,' she was muttering, like it was some kind of chant. 'Cleaning and burning! Cleaning and burning!'

I called out to her. 'Hello!' (I shouted it in case she was a bit deaf.) Twice I shouted it. She just put her arm over her face as if I was threatening to hit her. As if I could from the bank!

'Only being friendly,' I shouted.

She looked at me then and waved her arms about. She's got this grey old mac all wet at the cuffs and the hem. You'd think she'd wear something more practical for the river.

'All right then, *don't* speak!' I said because I was really fed up with all these non-speaking people in my life. And I gave her one of my Looks. The sort of Look I gave to Jem before he died.

But then she gave me a Look back! Really fierce. You wouldn't think anyone so old could have such fierce blue eyes. You'd think they'd have faded by now. And she muttered something long and dark. Or it sounded long and dark.

It might have been a spell.

When I got back to Teviotdale I found Megan making up a bed in the empty bedroom.

'What's going on?' I asked.

'We've got another boy coming,' Megan said. 'His name's Sam.'

I didn't tell them about the River Woman. Not then.

MEGAN'S DIARY

A new child arrives today. He's eight and his name's Sam. His social worker, Louise, visited last week and told me something about him. Sam's father left home two weeks ago. His mother's pregnant and says she can't cope. I saw a photo of Sam. He's small and wears specs though Louise says he's almost blind in one eye. Also a bit lame. I think his father beat him up when he was little. Sam's got an older brother, Peter, but he's gone off to London with the father. Louise says that Sam worships Peter but there may be what she calls 'letter box contact'.

I hate that phrase. It makes me think that the letter box

is like a kind of disembodied mouth and you keep hoping words will fall through it. Words like 'love' and 'see you soon' ands 'take care'. And when the mouth stays shut you really feel disappointed. I've seen children sitting on the bottom step of the stairs and crying because that letter box mouth hasn't opened. Still, I know letters are better than nothing. Louise says she's hoping Sam's mother will visit once a week and that Sam will be able to go home – maybe when the new baby's born.

Chapter Three

I WISH IT WAS A GIRL. A girl about my age who I could *talk* to. Instead we've got Sam. Or you could say we've got a frightened rabbit because that's what he looked like when he arrived.

I know what it's like, of course. Even when you've met the foster mum before – and they usually fix that – and even if you've visited the house and seen the room you're going to have, you still feel really spaced out. I think it must be like going to a strange country and you don't know the language or where the lavatory is or what's the time for dinner. Like that.

Me, I try to look as if there's nothing to it. I try to imagine I'm a posh, well-travelled lady who's used to going from hotel to hotel. So I dump my things in my room, and I put my Walkman on really loud to drown out all the sickly feelings. It doesn't get any better though. Mrs Nobes says if you keep practising something it gets easier. I bet Mrs Nobes has never been in care. I bet she's had one cosy home for ever and ever.

Sam's eight. His social worker, Louise, brought him. He had all his gear in a black bin liner and he was hanging on to this disgusting looking ted. Once upon a time it might have been a blue ted. Now it's a dirty grey smelly ted. Its ears look as if a dog has chewed them.

'And what's your ted called?' Megan asked him and Sam said, 'Erasmus.' I ask you, where did he get a name like that?

All Sam's clothes look too big for him. Hand-me-downs, I suppose. There must be something wrong with his eyes because he wears specs with real pebble lenses and he's got one leg shorter than the other, so he walks funny.

And he eats! He eats and eats and eats!

Megan likes us all to sit round the kitchen table for supper. It's a drag. I like mine on a tray in front of the telly, but Megan thinks we'll be more of a family if we all eat together. And we have to be polite and say 'Please will you pass the potatoes' and things like that. It's a House Rule.

Not that Sam could know that yet and maybe Megan didn't quite like to tell him on his first night. So we all watched while he stuffed his mouth. *All* the left-over potatoes. *All* the bread and butter. *Three* helpings of rhubarb crumble. And then he licked the bowl.

I was about to say something like 'Doesn't your mum feed you at home?' but Megan must have read my mind because she gave me one of her warning looks. So I didn't. I gave her a Look back, but she just grinned at me. Megan seems immune to my Looks. I'm glad really. I don't want Megan to crumple up and die.

And then, when there was absolutely nothing left to eat, you know what Sam did? He fell asleep! Right there at the table. His little head just went nod, nod, nod, and he was asleep. If there'd been any crumble and custard left in his bowl he'd have put his head in it.

Megan carried him into the sitting room and tucked him up on the sofa which meant we couldn't watch telly. Sam's smelly ted – Erasmus – had fallen on the floor so I thought I'd do something really nice and kind and wash him. So I took him into the bathroom and filled up the basin with some bath bubbles and stuck him in. I tried scrubbing him a bit with the nail brush and using the soap on his ears. He went all fat and bloated in the water and a bit of stuffing came out of his tummy. Anyway, then I squeezed and squeezed and squeezed the water out of him – he looked all kind of limp and skinny then – and stuck him on the radiator.

I thought Megan would be pleased with me and I'd get into her good books again after that fight with Raymond. But it seems I can't do anything right because when Sam woke up, about two hours later, he screamed the house down for his ted and everyone began hunting for it and suddenly I didn't quite like to say what I'd done, because he wasn't nearly dry. He was all soggy and horrible.

Sam lay face down on the floor and screamed and screamed. Whenever anyone went near him he kicked them. His specs got all blurred up with his tears. It was awful.

And then Megan found ted. She held him up by one soggy ear. She just said, 'Anna?' Nothing else, just 'Anna?'

I felt a bit tearful myself then, but I know how *not* to cry. You just blink very hard and swallow a couple of times, as if you're swallowing down the tears and you keep your teeth clenched tight. So I did all that and I didn't cry.

And then something really surprising happened. Megan burst out laughing. Even Raymond gave something like a giggle. And then Megan gave me a hug and said, 'I know you thought you were being kind, Anna.' And that made me feel even more like crying, though I don't know why.

Actually Erasmus *did* look very funny. The only person who didn't think he looked funny was Sam. He'd stopped screaming when Megan found his ted; now he was just sitting on the floor, sobbing.

'I'll put him in the tumble dryer,' Megan said. 'He'll be ready for you by bedtime.'

So Erasmus went in the dryer and Sam sat on the kitchen floor in front of it, sucking his thumb and waiting. And when Erasmus came out of the drier he looked quite clean and fluffy and I felt quite proud of myself. Sam just said, 'He doesn't smell the same.'

There's no pleasing some folk.

I thought I'd made things OK with Megan again, but then she found my torn shirt and jeans. I did it after the fight with Raymond. I never mean to do it. Somehow I just find myself with scissors in my hand cutting and tearing. And I carry on until something tight inside me stops feeling tight. This time there wasn't much left of my shirt and the jeans had big holes in them so I shoved them under my bed.

Megan said, 'Oh, Anna! I thought you'd stopped doing

that. You must have been feeling very angry.'

And I thought, well maybe I was. Maybe that was the tight feeling. Only it wasn't just because of Raymond or because of being sent to my room, it was more as if I wanted to rip up my life. Rip it up and start again. Start again back with my mum, that is.

Megan says we may be able to patch the jeans and if I like I can choose some really funky bits of material to patch them with. But the shirt has had it. Megan says I don't have any more clothing allowance from the social until next month. Boo hoo.

Came back from school along the river path again. And *she* was there! The River Woman. She'd made a bonfire on the bank. It lit up her face so she looked quite wild. Today she was wearing a kind of old tam o'shanter on her head. It looked dirtier than Sam's ted (before I washed him, that is). Lots of the other kids, including Gemma Ford, were trying to get close to the bonfire but the River Woman had this big nobbly stick and she shook it at them. Most of them just laughed, but they went away.

'I think she may be a witch,' I said to Gemma. I'd really like Gemma to be my best friend because I don't have one, but Gemma's already got a best friend. Andrea Lloyd in 8T. Still, she may get tired of her. I'm going to keep trying.

Anyway, Gemma just laughed and said, 'Oh, she's just a nutty old bag. Probably lives in a cardboard box.'

I didn't say anything. I mean if you want someone to be your best friend it's not a good idea to disagree with them first thing, is it? So I just said, 'Oh,' in a way that could mean yes, I agree, or no, I don't. And then I asked her if she'd like to come and have tea at my house. (It felt funny calling it 'my' house. I've never done that before.) But Gemma just looked at me as if I was nutty, too, and said, thanks, but no thanks. I don't think she's one of those non-talking people because I've heard her and Andrea gabbing away at break-time.

Miss Holland stopped me outside school today. She's Raymond's form teacher.

'Raymond hasn't been to school for two days now,' she said. 'Is he ill?'

I mumbled something about Raymond being unlikely to tell anyone if he was well or ill because he doesn't speak, but Miss Holland just looked very confused and said, 'Well, will you give this note to . . . to . . .'

'My foster carer,' I said, because I hate the way people get all embarrassed and don't know whether to say 'your mum' or 'your foster mum' or sometimes, 'the lady who looks after you'.

I didn't really want to take the note at all, but she'd got me so riled that I just snatched it from her and ran off.

Still, I don't think I'll give it to Megan. I don't want to be a tell-tale. Besides, there might be a time when I want to bunk off school, too.

Chapter Four

RAYMOND. RAYMOND. RAYMOND. It's amazing how someone who doesn't speak can become the centre of attention. I tried it myself one morning. Not talking, that is. By lunch-time I was almost bursting. I was like a paper bag so full of chips (words) that they were all spilling out.

I've had an important thought about words. It's this. If you don't say what you're thinking *to* someone, then all your thoughts get clogged up and soggy, like a newspaper does when you're turning it into papier mâché. (We did that in art last week.) Either that or you have a really good thought and it flies off, quick as a butterfly, and you never get it back again.

Anyway, I suppose you could say that Raymond has been just a little more talkative if you count three words all put together as talking. It's an improvement on 'yep' and 'naw'. And a big improvement on a grunt.

The thing is, I like Raymond really. I like it when he grins. Which isn't often. He's all closed up like a snail in a shell, but when he pops his head out and grins, you can't help but grin back.

I gave him the note from Miss Holland yesterday. Got a grunt by way of a thank you.

'You've been bunking off, haven't you?' I said.

A shrug.

'Where d'you go, then?'

'About.'

I don't know why I bother to ask really, because I know where Raymond goes. He goes to the river. If this was *The Wind in the Willows*, Raymond would be Ratty. Not that he's got a boat to go messing about in, like Ratty has. But in the book Ratty says that the river's his brother and sister, his aunts and his friend and I think that's what the river is to Raymond. And I wish I could go along the river with Raymond because I think he knows things about it that no one else does.

'You'd better watch it,' I said. 'I heard Megan say you've got a Review coming up soon.'

Another shrug but I could tell he was bothered because he bent down and hid his face in Toby-dog's curly coat.

'I'll go tomorrow,' he said. Wow! Three words!

Reviews are something you're always having if you're a kid in care. Reviews and reports. I hate them. Social workers, foster carers, teachers, the Children's Panel, they're all making notes on you and deciding what's going to happen to you and even though they sometimes ask you what *you*'d like, what you'd like often isn't what you get.

Actually, Raymond's been more shut in his snail-shell this week because of Sam. I think Sam's fixated on Raymond. He follows him everywhere. The other day he went into Raymond's room without asking if he could come in. That's against House Rules. Megan says we must all have our privacy. Anyway, when she told Sam that, he just squatted outside Raymond's door for *hours* and of course Raymond never invited him in.

I can't say I blame him. Sam's a pain. Sometimes he eats so much he makes himself sick. I was having a moan about it to Megan in the kitchen when I found there wasn't a single tub of yoghurt left in the fridge and the biscuit tin had nothing but crumbs in it.

Megan said, 'Sam's very homesick. He's got this really empty feeling inside him and he's trying to fill it up.'

Well, I understand that, but he's not the only one with an empty feeling.

Anyway, Sam has an older brother of his own. I know because Sam had a letter from him postmarked London and he carried it about with him all day until it was looking so crumpled and food stained, Megan suggested he put it under his pillow. Maybe Sam thinks Raymond can be a kind of replacement big brother.

All Raymond ever says to him is 'shove off'. But maybe that's what big brothers often say to their kid brothers. Maybe Sam is used to it. It doesn't seem to put him off. Sam has nightmares, too. Wakes everyone up with his screaming. Megan's looking really fed-up.

MEGAN'S DIARY

Who'd be a foster mum? It's been the most up and down sort of day. It began with a down. I was up half the night with Sam. First he was sick. Which meant changing all the sheets. Then he had a nightmare. And then he wet the bed. Which meant changing all the sheets again. So this morning I was really tired and fed up. Had to remind myself that there have *been good times.*

Poor Sam. He's finding it very hard. So many losses all at once. I imagine he's glad his dad has left home. From what Louise told me it seems his dad was ashamed of Sam being a bit handicapped with his leg and his eyesight. Was forever taunting him and bullying him. And now there's this new baby on the way. Sam must feel his mum just doesn't want him.

Sorry for Sam as I am – because I think he could be a dear little fellow – I'm still finding it hard going. You wouldn't think, when you look at that fostering magazine, Be My Parent, *and see all those children smiling out at you and looking so lovely you want to bring them all home, that it would be as difficult as this. A twenty-four-hour job. Now I know what they mean when they say a child has 'challenging behaviour'. For challenging behaviour read temper tantrums, bed wetting, lying, stealing, breaking your furniture, breaking your heart.*

And of course they – the social workers – do warn you. And you get training that tells you what you might expect and it all helps, but somehow in the middle of the night when you're mopping up the sick – it doesn't.

I've had to look back in this diary to remember the children we've had and how sometimes there was a kind of happy ending – they went back home or got adopted by a really nice family – and sometimes there was a sad ending. I think of Polly who went back home but within a month was back in care. And I think of Jamie who comes to see me sometimes and who lives with the Bennetts over in Drummond Street and has just started college. I've got photographs of children going back seven years now. It makes me feel better, looking at them. And it makes me feel better writing this diary. Saying how I feel.

Chapter Five

GEMMA FORD walked home from school with me today. There was no sign of the River Woman, just the blackened remains of her bonfire. The river was quite high today. I like it like that when it's all urgent and rushing.

Gemma said, 'What's it like where you live?'

'It's nice,' I said. 'We're allowed to stay up really late.' (We're not really, but I didn't want Gemma feeling sorry for me.)

'Don't you miss your mum and dad? Your real mum and dad that is?' she asked.

For a minute I almost forgot my story about being abandoned and I was just going to tell her about Mum being a famous actress. Instead I put on my tragic face and said, 'Well, I never knew them. Being abandoned, you know.'

'Oh,' said Gemma and I could tell she thought it was really romantic. I know girls at school who wish their real mums and dads *weren't* their real mums and dads.

'And then you were found and taken care of,' said Gemma.

'Yep,' I said. I was beginning to feel like Raymond, not wanting to talk but wanting to keep Gemma beside me.

We'd reached the remains of the bonfire now so I said, 'Where d'you think the River Woman lives?'

'I dunno,' said Gemma, 'I've never really thought about it.'

'We could follow her one day,' I said. 'See where she goes.'

'OK,' Gemma said, all casual-like and as if we'd often done things together. I took it as a pledge. A pledge of everlasting friendship. And anyone would get bored with that Andrea Lloyd. Andrea Lloyd hasn't got a single magical thought in her entire body.

Actually, although I didn't say so to Gemma, the idea of following the River Woman gave me the shivers. It made me remember that in *The Wind in the Willows* there's a place beyond the river called 'The Wild Wood'. I hope that isn't where the River Woman lives. There's evil weasels in the wild wood. Horrid faces peering at you out of dark holes.

When I got back to Teviotdale, who should be on the doorstep but Miss Holland. I didn't really want to go in, but she'd already seen me. More trouble.

Megan's Diary

I'm sure, given time, things will improve here. It's just that Anna, Raymond and Sam don't seem to have settled down together at all.

Anna. Oh Anna! Too much imagination for her own good, that one. The stories she tells about her mum! They change almost every other week. First her mum's a famous actress – on tour if you please. Or else she was abandoned on the doorstep. Less than a week old. Wrapped in wonderful blankets and put on a doorstep in the snow. You have to admit that Anna's good at embroidering a tale. I mean she wouldn't be abandoned on a nice warm summer's night, would she? It would have to be snow. The truth is, Anna's mum has been in gaol for theft. Before that she was in a rehab unit for people who drink too much. Now she's just missing. Gone without trace. And Anna's dad? Goodness only knows.

You can't blame Anna for not wanting to admit the truth. Not wanting to know it really. It's too painful. Hopefully there will come a time when she'll be able to look at it and accept it – and maybe grow from that acceptance.

I think Anna is keen to make friends with Raymond but they're like chalk and cheese those two. Anna can't stop talking. Raymond can't begin. That makes Anna so frus-

trated they end up quarrelling. Or worse still fighting.

All in all, the last thing I needed was Raymond's teacher, Miss smiley-smiley Holland on my doorstep telling me that Raymond hadn't been at school for three days now and had I had the note she'd given to Anna?

No, of course I hadn't. I don't much care for Miss Holland. Somehow she's over-cheerful. I asked her in and offered her a cup of tea. Just as I'd poured it out, Raymond himself appeared. Went bright red when he saw Miss Holland and looked about to bolt. If it hadn't been for Toby leaping all over him, he probably would have done.

I felt really disappointed in Raymond. I admit, I've got a soft spot for him. He reminds me of my kid brother. And then there's something brave about Raymond. Whenever I try to give Raymond a hug he just stands there, very stiff with his face turned away from me. It makes me sad.

'There's some tea in the pot, Raymond,' I said, calm as could be. 'You'll know why Miss Holland's here.'

'Ummm.'

'Perhaps you can explain why you haven't been at school?' says Miss Holland, with that over-sweet smile of hers.

'Bored,' said Raymond.

Miss Holland flushed a little at that.

'That's not really a good enough excuse, Raymond,' I said. 'Where have you been when you've not been at school?' (Of course I knew the answer.)

'Down by the river.'

'Well,' said Miss Holland, 'I trust we can expect you at school tomorrow morning?'

'Yes, miss,' said Raymond, scuffing his feet. His muddy feet.

'And,' said Miss Holland, 'seeing you've spent so much time by the river and seeing you're behind on your homework, you can write me a nice long essay all about the river, can't you, Raymond?'

'Yes, miss.'

'Raymond,' I said when she'd gone. 'You know you've

got a Review coming up, don't you? The Children's Panel won't be too happy to hear of you missing school. They might think I'm not looking after you properly.' To myself I was thinking, 'And they might move you to another carer.'

And then Raymond looked at me. Really looked at me. Proper eye contact.

'Well, you are,' he said.

So I gave him a hug and he didn't exactly hug me back, but he let himself be hugged.

Who'd be a foster mum? ME!!!

Chapter Six

I TOLD MEGAN I was going to an after-school club and Megan said didn't I have a note about it and I said yes, I had, only I'd left it at school. Megan said, 'Well, I'll trust you then,' and I felt rather bad, particularly after all that stuff with the note from Miss Holland. But I knew Megan would never let me go down the river with Gemma, following the River Woman. I haven't mentioned the River Woman to anyone in the house. I know what they'd say. 'Stories, Anna! Stories!'

Gemma and I had arranged to meet by the bridge. You can often see the River Woman from there without her seeing you.

'What if she doesn't go *anywhere*?' Gemma asked. 'What if she just stays by the river for hours? Maybe even *sleeps* by it? How long are we going to wait to find out?'

'She doesn't sleep by it,' I said, 'because I've seen her go down the track. She's often gone when we come out of school. I don't think she likes children.'

Gemma shivered a bit when I said that.

'So she may have gone when we get to the bridge?' Gemma said. I thought she sounded rather hopeful.

'She may,' I said. But she hadn't.

She was packing some junk in an old builder's bag, head down as usual, intent on what she was doing.

'She's ready to go,' I said to Gemma. 'Let's go down the steps. Just keep chatting as if we haven't seen her.'

'What if she sees *us*?' asked Gemma.

'She's too busy dragging that bag,' I said. It looked heavy.

'Perhaps it's got a body in it,' said Gemma.

I was quite impressed by that. I didn't think Gemma had much imagination. The stories she did for school were yawn-yawn boring. Perhaps the river had got to her.

There'd been a lot of rain so the river was quite high. More rain looked on the way because the sky was all dark as if it was in a really fed-up mood. The willows were shifting uneasily and when the River Woman passed *The Pigeon Post* tree, all the pigeons took off in a great wave as if they'd heard some really disturbing news.

For a moment I thought maybe Gemma was right and the River Woman *did* have a body in her bag. But then I remembered how I'd seen her packing things in it before – bottles, old car tyres, tins and empty gas cylinders.

'It's all right,' I told Gemma. 'She just likes junk.'

'And she doesn't like children,' Gemma said.

'If she turns on us, we'll run,' I said. 'She's ancient. She'd never catch us.'

Gemma didn't look very convinced, but she followed me down the steps onto the river bank and we started walking behind the River Woman.

It wasn't easy because the River Woman was going so slowly. Every now and again she'd stop, put the sack down and then stomp on again. We had to stop, too. We pretended to be watching the swans. Three times Gemma pretended to be tying up the laces on her trainers. Once we sat on the wall and undid our school bags as if looking for something.

The thing about the river is that you can't walk along it all the way. Here and there the path takes you onto the road and then you have to zig-zag down side roads to find the river again. I knew the way the River Woman was going would take us onto the road. Maybe then she'd go to her house. If she had a house, that is. Somehow I imagined a cave was more likely. Only I didn't know of any handy caves. I thought I wouldn't mention caves to Gemma because she was looking more scared by the minute. I decided to hold her hand and she didn't resist. Her hand was all hot and sweaty, the way your hands go when you're scared.

As I expected, the River Woman took the path that led to the road. But she left the bag at the site that looked as if she'd had a bonfire there before. We'd got a bit too close to her by then and could hear her muttering to herself.

'What's she whispering?' Gemma whispered, as though whispers were catching.

'Probably "Cleaning and burning. Cleaning and burning." That's what I've heard her say.'

'I don't like the sound of it,' said Gemma.

There wasn't time to talk any more because, without the bag, the River Woman began walking quickly. She had a strange walk as if her feet weren't really at home on land. It made me think of toddlers learning to walk.

We were suddenly on the road with lots of traffic whizzing by. We almost lost her then because the traffic lights changed, but I saw her go down the back of Tescos and off to the right. It seemed to be right, left, right, left, right, after that.

'We'll never find our way back,' Gemma moaned. I was beginning to worry about that myself. But very soon we were by the river again, with the River Woman hurrying ahead. Only this part of the river was very different from *our* part, the stretch of the river between school and home. Our part is flat and the houses – including Megan's – all overlook it. There's a block of flats for old people as well as the ordinary houses. You can see people and buses and things going by on the bridge and there's the pizza place at the top of the steps. And lots and lots of people walk along our stretch of the river. They walk their dogs. They carry their shopping home. They fish there. They walk home from school. So it's a *friendly* stretch of river. Even the swans and the pigeons make it seem friendly.

But this stretch of river was quite different. The path became just a narrow track sloping downwards. There were no houses, just trees. Crowds of trees, making the place seem really dark.

'It's like the Wild Wood!' I said to Gemma. I could feel my hand just as hot as hers now.

'The what?' whispered Gemma.

33

'The Wild Wood,' I said, 'like in *The Wind in the Willows.*'

'Is that on telly?' Gemma asked.

'It's a book,' I said.

Then the River Woman dodged and was away, somewhere among the trees.

'Let's go back,' hissed Gemma.

'Not yet, not yet!' I said.

Suddenly we found ourselves stumbling on gravestones! They stood or leant at all angles. Some of them half out of the earth. Others broken or propped up against a tree. It wasn't like the cemetery near the church which is all neat and tidy and where a gardener comes and cuts the grass round the edges and people visit and put fresh flowers on the gravestones. This was a kind of forgotten cemetery. A cemetery for people no one remembered any more. Maybe, I thought, people who had lost their families. Abandoned people.

I was ready to run for it then. I thought that at any minute we'd start seeing eyes looking at us out of those broken graves like the eyes in the Wild Wood and I thought that wherever the River Woman was going, I didn't want to know any more. We didn't speak, Gemma and I. We just looked at each other and turned round, ready to try and find our way back.

Then we heard it. A splashing noise.

'Maybe she's drowned,' Gemma whispered. And we both hesitated.

'We'd better look,' I said.

So we crept through the trees, trying not to make any noise which was really difficult because there were all sorts of twigs and old leaves and things on the ground. Fortunately the sound of the river covered up the sound of our feet.

The River Woman was *in* the river. Naked! In January! All her old and tatty clothes lay in a bundle on the bank. It was ever so cold but she just stood there, splashing herself all over and singing!

And we just stood and stared, Gemma and I. I don't think we could have moved even if we'd wanted to.

The funny thing was that the River Woman looked much younger without her clothes. It was almost as if she had not only taken off her clothes but taken off years and years. Her hair almost looked golden instead of white. I don't know *what* she was singing, but it sounded somehow . . . happy. And suddenly I thought of how Ratty and Mole meet the god Pan by the river, playing his pipes. Only of course Pan was half-man, half-goat, not an old woman who went about (usually) in a pair of wellies and an old mac. So I didn't mention Pan to Gemma in case she laughed at me.

Not that either of us felt like laughing just then. We just made off. Stumbling back through the gravestones, not caring how much noise we made, and on back to the road. If it hadn't been for the glimpse of Tescos and the sound of traffic, I'm not too certain we'd have *found* the road again. But we did.

Gemma said, 'Are you going to tell your mum – I mean your foster mum?'

'No,' I said, 'are you going to tell yours?'

'No,' said Gemma. 'Let's keep it our secret.'

I felt that really made us Best Friends. A shared secret.

Chapter Seven

RAYMOND'S ECO MAP

1. ME Raymond Eccles   2. TODAY IS Monday,

3. I AM 10 YEARS OLD   4. MEMORIES

This is my birth home.
22 Alnwick St
Edinburgh
My mum lives here.

5. MEMORIES

This is my first foster home. I first came here when I was 7. I lived with Mr + Mrs CLUNY and daughter Tracy.

6. MY SOCIAL WORKER IS

Alison BYNG,
She moves me about and helps me
see my mum.

7. I NOW LIVE AT

21 Teviotdale Place
Edinburgh.
I live with Megan, Anna, Sam and Toby.

8. HOW I GOT HERE

The Children's Panel put me in care,

9. FRIENDS

Toby-dog.

10. WHY AM I HERE?

Because my mum can't look after me and because my dad left home and my step-dad doesn't like me.

11. BROTHERS AND SISTERS

I have a half-sister, Mary.

12. I WORRY ABOUT	13. I DREAM ABOUT
Nothing	going home.

14. I FEEL	15. SCHOOL
nothing	I miss my old school

16. THINGS I LIKE TO DO	17. THINGS THAT BUG ME
Playing by the river.	House Rules (Sam)

18. MY FAVOURITE COLOUR	19. MY LEAST FAVOURITE
Browny-grey like the river	Orange-my bedroom walls.

MY RIVER *by Raymond Eccles, Form 6N*

THE NAME OF MY RIVER is the Water of Leith which is a very funny name for a river. Other rivers are called rivers, like the River Thames (in London) or the River Mersey (in Liverpool). I like the name of my river because it has a nice sound.

If you look at the river on a map, it is like a long riggling green snake running through the city. Of course it is not really green. It is all colours of grey and brown. More browns than in a paint box.

The river is 35 km long. It starts in the Pentland hills and goes out into the sea at the port of Leith. Maybe it should be called The Water of the Pentland Hills.

It is my ambishun to walk from the beginning to the end of the river but I am not allowed to. I will do it one day.

There are lots of things you can do by the river. If you have wellies you can wade in and make dams with the stones. If you have a fishing rod (I haven't) you can fish for trout. There are some good trees to clime. You can take your dog for a long walk like I do with Toby. You can have a picnic.

There are swans on the river. They have just had a baby. It isn't wite like its parents. It is grey and fluffy. There are a lot of ducks too. They have green velvet heads. And there is a heron. The heron has very long legs which it lifts very carefully one after the other. It can stand on one leg for ages and ages. The heron is a tall bird and very watchful. If I was a bird I would like to be a heron. Sometimes there are squirrels on the bank of the river.

People say that sometimes browkin harted lovers stand on the bridge and throw their diamond rings into the river but I have never found one.

In summer the willow trees are very pretty. They lean over the river as if they want to dip themselves in it. There are lots of bluebells and some brambles. Toby likes eating brambles and so do I. We don't like the nettles.

There is an old woman who tries to keep the river clean because people are bad and throw a lot of junk into the river. Sometimes I help her a bit and she smiles at me. She doesn't smile at anyone else. I don't blame her.

What I like most about the river is that it is very change-ful. Sometimes it is slow and quiet like an old dog you can pat. And other days it is wild and feerce and could brake down walls and maybe even houses.

But the river is always there.

THE END

Quite good, Raymond, but very poor spelling.
Write the following in your work book. B

wriggling	*changeable*
ambition	*fierce*
climb	
broken hearted	*A baby swan is called a cygnet.*
break	

MEGAN'S DIARY

'He looks very skinny!' That was the first thing Raymond's mum said when we met in the café. She said it accusingly and didn't wait for my answer.

'Are you getting enough to eat, Ray?' she asked him.

'Course,' Raymond said, scuffing his feet under the table.

This is the first time Raymond's mum, Dawn, has actually turned up. We're meant to meet once a month. The first time she phoned and said she wasn't well. The second time she just didn't turn up.

When I woke this morning my first thought was, 'I can't bear it if she doesn't come.'

I can tell what it does to Raymond just by his body language. The tension in him is almost electric. You could strike a match off his skin, he's so uptight. It's impossible for him to sit still. He winds and unwinds his legs, hunches his shoulders, kicks things. And his face is all tight. He looks as if he's holding on to his heart, squeezing that tight, too. The night before a meeting he never sleeps well. His light's on past midnight. And in the morning he can barely eat any breakfast.

I hate the café where we meet – or don't as the case might be – but it's the only place Dawn will agree to. I suppose it's handy for her. And I suppose it's neutral territory. But for all that it's one of those bleak cafés that should have shut down years ago only its owners can't somehow be bothered.

I think they do breakfasts for lorry drivers and maybe once they've done that they're exhausted for the rest of the day. There's steamy glass windows at the front of the café and usually someone smearing a tired mop over the floor. Mostly there's just the one worn-out waitress which means the tables don't get cleared properly and you have to pile up the plates with dried up fried egg and tomato sauce on them and dump the tinfoil ashtrays overflowing with butts. Behind the counter there's a display of stale-looking buns and scones and sandwiches with limp lettuce hanging out of them. The biscuits are in packs so there's a chance they're not stale.

When we went there last month, Raymond had a present for his mum. It was a small bowl he'd whittled out of a piece of driftwood he'd found in the river.

We sat at a table by the window with Raymond rubbing a hole in the steam so he could see out. And we waited and waited and waited.

'Maybe she's got the date wrong,' I suggested. I felt really angry with her. How could you disappoint a kid like Raymond? And I was angry with myself for feeling angry because a major part of being a foster mum is to understand and accept the child's birth mother.

'Probably she couldn't get away,' Raymond said.

I knew what he meant by that. The problem is Raymond's step-dad who doesn't really want to know Raymond exists. Would probably prefer it if he didn't. He was always beating Raymond with a belt while his own daughter, Mary, was kissed and cuddled and spoilt rotten. 'Probably couldn't get away' meant that there'd been a row and Raymond's step-dad had threatened to leave if Dawn went out to see Raymond.

We waited an hour, playing noughts and crosses and hangman to pass the time and afterwards, in an attempt to cheer Raymond up, we went to a cartoon show. Only neither of us found much to laugh at that afternoon and under cover of darkness I could see Raymond wiping his eyes.

This time I was probably as tense as Raymond. Both of us were trying not to get our hopes up. But we'd only just got ourselves cups of tea and settled at the table when she arrived.

Raymond's smile! I'm ashamed to write this, but I thought, 'She doesn't deserve that smile' and then, 'Will Raymond ever smile at me like that?'

She was all in a flustery hurry and full of those sorts of questions people ask when they don't really want any answers.

To Raymond: 'You're doing all right then?'

To me: 'He's behaving himself, is he?'

I went to get her a coffee, taking my time so she and Raymond could be alone together, if only for a few minutes. When I got back to the table I could see things weren't going well. Dawn was chain-smoking and Raymond was slouched in his seat. When I looked out of the window I could see why.

A car with its engine running had drawn up outside. There was a man and a little girl in it. Raymond's step-dad and Mary, his half sister.

'I thought he'd like to see his little sister,' Dawn was saying. 'I mean she'd come in if I asked her. She talks about you a lot, Ray.'

'I suppose she's got my room,' said Raymond.

'Well, there was no point in her staying in that little box room, was there?' said Dawn. 'Not now she's bigger. She'd like to see you, Ray, really she would. Shall I fetch her in?'

The engine revving outside seemed to grow louder and louder. More and more impatient.

Raymond just shook his head.

'Stubborn,' said Dawn. 'He always was stubborn. I suppose you find him stubborn, too, don't you?'

'Raymond knows what he wants,' I said.

'And anyway, that room's big enough to share,' said Dawn. 'When you come home.'

'If,' said Raymond. 'If, not when. If he goes.'

Dawn got all tearful then. 'You don't know what it's like for me,' she said – to me rather than Raymond. 'He's not a bad man, my Stan. It's just Raymond's always got on the wrong side of him, haven't you, Raymond? And he and Mary were always fighting. I had the worst of it all. Me. Piggy in the middle.'

Outside the car engine quietened and then Stan began tooting the horn.

'I gotta go,' said Dawn, 'but I'll see you next month, darling. You know I love you, don't you? Be good now.'

'I've brought you this,' said Raymond, and he gave her the whittled bowl. He'd wrapped it up in tissue paper.

Dawn looked at it as if she didn't know what to do with it. She pushed it in the pocket of her coat, blew Raymond a kiss from the door and was gone.

Chapter Eight

W E'VE HAD AN EMERGENCY. I mean an Emergency Arrival! It was the middle of the night and I wasn't sleeping properly because I kept dreaming of the River Woman. How she looks in her everyday old mac and wellies, and how she looked when Gemma and I watched her bathing in the river. It feels funny when I say that, 'bathing in the river'. It's like what nymphs do in legends. Once I woke up thinking maybe she was a swan who's fallen in love with a mortal and now she was hunting in the river for her swan suit. Perhaps the real swans were her family, waiting for her. I read a story like that once.

Anyway, you think all kinds of daft things in the night. Or I do. And I couldn't get back to sleep. I was lying there on my back watching the lights from the occasional car flash across my ceiling like birds across the sky, and trying to work out whether the River Woman was somehow guarding us – all of us who live near the river – or if her 'cleaning and burning' sort of included us, all human-kind. We were to be cleared away. Put on a bonfire with the trash and then the river would be clean again, like at the beginning of the world.

Then I heard the phone go and the sound of Megan trying to go downstairs very quietly which isn't easy because there's a lot of creaky steps. Then lights came on and I heard a car drawing up outside. I looked at my Mickey Mouse alarm clock. 3 a.m! Whoever it was didn't ring the bell or anything. Megan just opened the door and in they came. One of the social workers with this boy.

I tucked myself in on the landing to see what was happening. There was a lot of whispering. I heard the social worker apologising because foster carers don't usually have more than two children, but this *was* an emergency and they hadn't been able to find anyone else. Then there was something about a fight and the police. The boy just stood there looking kind of wild with his clothes all torn and blood on his face. He was holding one arm across his chest as if it really hurt.

Just before Megan took them both off to the kitchen, he looked up at me and our eyes met. At least I think they did. He looked a bit as if he'd seen a ghost. It is just possible that I may have seen the love of my life. If you can have one, that is. But I intend to try. I'm not going to give up on love, like people do when they get old and tired.

I went back to bed then because they shut the kitchen door and I couldn't hear any more. I tried to stay awake so maybe I'd hear more but I fell asleep. When I came down-stairs this morning, there was a guitar in the hall and Megan was clearing up in the kitchen. She was still in her dressing gown which she never is because she usually takes Sam to school. The First Aid Box was still out and she was shoving clothes in the washing machine. Jeans and a blood-stained shirt. Before I could ask any questions, Megan said, 'Lay the table will you, Anna. I'm running late.'

'Has someone come?' I asked, all innocent. 'I heard voices last night.'

'Not now, Anna. Not now,' Megan said.

So I laid the table and made myself some sandwiches for my lunch box and *at last*, when we were all sitting down for breakfast, Megan said, 'We've got a newcomer in the house. His name is Brent.'

I really liked the name. It's kind of short and strong and maybe American.

'He's having a lie-in this morning,' Megan said, 'but you'll meet him after school. We'll have a welcome supper.'

Megan had a welcome supper for me when I first came. It was fish fingers and chips which normally I adore, but I couldn't eat anything because I was feeling so strange. So not-myself. You'd have thought those fish fingers had bones in them the way they nearly choked me.

'I never had a welcome supper,' said Sam.

'You did,' I told him, 'only you've forgotten because you stuffed your face so much you were sick.'

'I never,' said Sam.

Sam is amazing. I think he's got a memory with a 'delete' button on it like the one on Mr Thomas's computer. When Sam does something naughty he just presses the delete button in his head and it never happened.

'You're always being sick,' said Raymond.

'Oh, he can speak,' I said, because I don't think Raymond has spoken two words to me all week. And what makes me really mad is that when he *does* speak it's a major event and Megan acts as if she's been given a bunch of flowers or a birthday present.

'Shut it,' said Raymond.

'That was a really long sentence,' I said, trying to look cool and mocking, though honestly, I could have hit him!

'I was never sick,' Sam said again.

'You will be if you eat any more toast,' I said.

And then of course Sam started crying and Megan said, 'Please! Can we start the day by being friendly.'

It was a bit late for that. We all had to dash to school. Megan just put her coat on over her pyjamas and I forgot my sandwiches but Megan brought them round while I was in maths.

When I got home Brent was lying full leggy length on the sofa, *smoking*! Now if there's one House Rule Megan's really fierce about, it's smoking.

'You're not allowed,' I said.

Brent looked at me. He had these dark kind of gypsy eyes. Megan must have taken him to the doctor's or the hospital this morning because the cut above his eye had stitches in it and his left arm was in a sling.

'Who cares?' he said.

'Megan does,' I said. 'A lot. It's Numero One of the House Rules.'

'Megan's out,' Brent said. 'Shopping.'

'She'll smell it,' I said. 'As soon as she walks in.' And I shoved open the windows even though it felt like the coldest day of the year.

'Who cares,' said Brent again.

I thought he looked like a wounded warrior, lying there all dark and broody. Well, mostly dark and broody. I don't suppose warriors had streaks of pink dye in their hair. Maybe they painted their shields instead. I don't suppose warriors had twitchy legs either. Sort of nervous legs. Long but nervous.

'How long you been here, then?' he asked.

'Three months,' I said. 'This is my fourth foster home.'

'You difficult, then?' he said, grinning.

'I do magical thinking,' I said.

Brent grinned even more. 'You mean you tell porkies,' he said.

'I'm not too interested in facts,' I said, perching myself on the arm of a chair in the way I'd seen models do in photographs when they want to show off their legs. (I think my legs are my best feature – if you can call legs a feature.)

'I think the *real* truth is what you feel about things,' I said. I didn't want to tell him about *divine discontent* yet. I didn't think he was ready for it. But he has this wild look which I think means he probably has it, too. Divine discontent that is.

'Who cares,' he said again. I began to think he was never going to say anything else and that maybe it was my awful fate to live with people who either won't talk or who just say the same thing over and over again, like parrots do.

'So why are you here?' he asked, stubbing his cigarette out in one of Megan's plant pots. I was glad of a question, even if it wasn't an easy one.

'Abandoned,' I said. Megan keeps trying to hint that I should try telling the truth instead of telling stories. But it isn't *exactly* a story. Abandoned's how I feel.

'Oh yeah,' said Brent. 'In a cardboard box, I suppose, and left on the doorstep. You're the love-child of some rich heiress and one day she's coming back for you.'

'Actually,' I said, 'my mother's an actress. She's on tour at the moment.'

'Oh yeah?' said Brent.

'Well, why are you here?' I countered.

'What's it look like?' he said, pointing at his arm and the cut above his eye.

'Like you've been in a fight,' I said.

'You don't like facts,' he said. 'An alien got me on my way to bed.'

'I'd like to know what happened to you.'

'I've told you. An alien got me. An alien called Dad.'

'I'm sorry,' I said.'

'Who cares,' said Brent for the umpteenth time.

I wanted to say, 'I do. I care.' But I didn't dare. There was something about Brent that pushed you away from caring. Something that said *Keep Off! Keep Away! Trespassers will be punched on the nose.*

'Anyway, what's it like here?' he asked, and I knew he wanted to change the subject.

'It's OK,' I said, 'if you can put up with Sam and Raymond and a thousand and one House Rules and always someone wanting to *assess* how you're doing and writing it all down like your life might vanish if they didn't.'

'Well, I can vanish any time I like,' Brent said.

'You can?'

'Just try and show me a car I can't get in,' he said, lolling back on the sofa. 'Citroën. Porsche. BMW. Three minutes and I'm away. Brrrooomh!'

You know just for one strange minute Brent didn't look like a broody wounded warrior (only with pink stripes in his hair), he suddenly looked like Toad in *WITW*. Toad with his obsession for cars. Brrrooomh!

'Poop! Poop!' I said, without thinking, because that's what Toad says.

'What?' Brent was back to looking wild and handsome again.

'Nothing,' I said. 'Just a story I read about someone

mad on cars. Is that what you've done, then? Nicked cars?'

Brent went a bit red. I think I'd called his bluff. 'It's not what I've done,' he said. 'It's what I *could* do. Any time. Any time I wanted.'

And then Megan came in and said, 'Smoking, Brent!' in her very firm voice and she found the stub in the plant pot straight away.

Sometimes I think Megan has extra sensory perception.

Chapter Nine

A DISCOVERY! Brent talks! He can talk as much as I can, possibly more! Of course it didn't happen all at once. During the first few days here he was just sullen and broody. His social worker, Felicity, came one afternoon after school and I could hear bits of the conversation going on in the kitchen. Seems Brent was what they call 'out of control' and it had ended up with a violent fight with his dad. I think his dad is something like a professor. He sounds a bit of a bully to me. And as if he's always wanting Brent to be like him.

Brent is going to stay here until things calm down at home and they've had some help from a psychologist or someone. I hope it takes a long time. I hope Brent stays here for months and months and months.

Anyway, on Saturday Megan said Brent and I could go into town together. Brent hasn't been allowed out all week so he was really keen. Said he knew lots of good coffee bars and maybe he could go to the tattoo parlour. Megan said 'no' to that. It would need his parents' consent and Brent went all sulky again. I was glad Megan said no. I'm a bit squeamish about needles of any sort. Even watching someone else have an injection makes me feel pukey.

Anyway, Brent cheered up and said he might see some of his mates in town and Megan said that was OK, only we had to stay together and be back by five. Oh, I nearly forgot, of course Sam wanted to come with us. I think Sam has given up on Raymond and is trying to 'adopt' Brent as his big brother. For a moment I thought we might have to take him because he was limping after us looking really pathetic, clutching Erasmus and chewing his ear, the way he always does.

But then Megan said she would take Sam swimming.

'But I can't swim,' said Sam.

'That's all right,' said Megan. 'I've got some water wings. Put them on and you'll be fine. And anyway, I'll be with you and we'll stay in the shallow end.'

Of course Sam wanted to know if Erasmus could come too.

'Only if you want to drown him,' I said. But Megan frowned at me, so I said sorry and why not leave Erasmus by the window so he could be looking out for them when they came home and everyone thought that was a good idea. Phew!

So that was settled and Brent and I went off to catch the bus into town. Brent was wearing an old leather jacket and looking really trendy. I thought anyone seeing us might think we were girl- and boy-friend and I felt really chuffed sitting beside him up on the top deck of the bus. I could feel the warmth of his arm and it made me feel cosy and comfortable. Also, taking the odd peep at him, sideways, I could see he had these really long eyelashes. The sort of eyelashes girls have when they use loads of mascara.

It was a frosty, February day and all the buildings were looking kind of shiny and there were loads of people shopping in Princes Street so it felt buzzy and exciting and the bus climbed up The Mound and you could see the castle standing stark and proud on the hillside.

We got off by the library and then walked down this little curvy street that's got lots of shops with really funny names like *Wacky Kool Enterprises* and *Aha ha ha* (that's a jokes and tricks shop) and *Mr Wood's Fossils*. There's a shop that sells nothing but brushes and a big market place called Byzantium. It's got lots of smaller shops inside it and it's full of second-hand clothes and antiquey things and old records and books and you feel you're in another country when you're in there because it's so exotic. Or maybe in another century because some of the things are so old. Brent bought an ear-ring and a T-shirt. I didn't buy anything because I only had enough money for coffee and something to eat at lunch-time and I was already starving.

Then we walked down to what they call the Grass-market. There isn't a market there now, or only sometimes in the summer. But Megan says it used to be the place where they sold cattle and horses and that ages ago. Bonnie Prince Charlie's army marched through here on its way to battle. Anyway, no market and no grass either, but there's lots of cafés with tables outside even now, in the middle of winter. It was sunny-ish, so we sat outside one of the cafés and drank coffee and that's when Brent and I began talking. Really talking. About all the important things.

Of course it began in the usual way. Brent was smoking his roll-ups and I said, 'I suppose you know you're killing yourself.'

'Who cares!' he said. He doesn't say it as a question. He says it as a nobody-cares *fact*.

'Well,' I said, 'I expect your mum and dad would.' I was wondering who would care if I was killing myself with heroin or something. I thought maybe Megan would, but then maybe not for long.

'What they care about,' said Brent, 'is that I get tons of Highers and go to University and get a great job and earn lots of money.'

'Don't you want to do any of that?'

'How do I know what I want?' said Brent. 'But I want to make my own choices. The only time my dad really seems to like me is when I've done well at something. Got a good report or something. And all they want me to do is sit at home studying. "You've got to think of the future" they keep saying. Thing is, there's not much I *am* good at.'

He looked really miserable when he said that, so I reached out and held his hand and he didn't take it away. Or not at once.

'I bet there are things,' I said, 'and maybe things you don't even know about yet.'

'I'm good at mechanics,' said Brent. 'Anything wrong with a car engine and I can fix it.'

'Well, there you are then,' I said. (I thought I wouldn't

mention nicking cars in case it set him off boasting again, like Toad does.

'Doesn't count with my folks,' he said. 'What about yours? When you see them that is.'

I took a deep breath. 'Well, I don't actually. See them, that is.'

And Brent said, 'I'm sorry. You don't have to talk about it if you don't want to.'

And suddenly I did want to. I wanted to badly. So I told him all about how I'd never known my father and how this was my fourth foster home and how my mother drank and kept going into one of these rehab places and how now I didn't know where she was. I told him how my mum's sister, Janie, used to come and throw out all the bottles she found under the bed and in the cupboards and how she'd give us some money only as soon as she'd gone Mum would be down to the shop for more booze and how Janie got really angry and Mum told her to go away and never come back. And then she didn't. And I told him how Mum got more and more in debt until we were evicted from our flat and I told him how I hated thinking about it all and remembering and how I made up that she was an actress because that's what I wanted to be one day. And how I pretended I'd been abandoned because it sounded really romantic . . . and then I was quite out of breath and crying.

Then it was Brent's turn to hold my hand and he dug out this really disgusting hankie and I dried my eyes and blew my nose and somehow we both started laughing.

After that we went and ate these huge cheeseburgers and followed them with ice cream and went walking across the meadows and Brent showed off doing lots of cartwheels and I didn't mind him showing off at all.

Then we walked all the way home because we'd run out of money for the bus and Brent said, 'Maybe I'm lucky having my folks,' all thoughtful-like, and I said maybe he was and maybe he needed to tell them what he really thought and felt.

'I might try,' Brent said.

When we got back Megan said, 'You two look as if you've had a really good time.' And Brent said, 'Yes, we have.' I felt all glowy when he said that.

'I swam!' Sam said.

'Sam swam!' said Brent and we all laughed and began dancing round the kitchen singing 'Sam swam! Sam swam! Sam swam!' Sam joined in too, hopped about until his specs all steamed up. Maybe he's not such a bad kid.

I've told Gemma about Brent. She's seen him at school – though he's two forms up from us.

'He's really cool,' Gemma said. 'I wouldn't mind having a foster kid in our house if it was somone like Brent.'

'You might get a Sam,' I said. I hate being called 'a foster kid' as though I wasn't quite normal or had a wart on the end of my nose or two extra ears. Still, I could tell Gemma was quite jealous and I was pleased about that, even though that wasn't very nice of me. But then I'm often jealous of Gemma, so it made a change. I'm jealous of her hair. She's got long red hair. It's the colour of autumn leaves. And I'm jealous of her family and that she *always* gets B+ or A for her English homework and I never quite manage an A because Mrs Nobes says I go off on side-tracks and I ought to *plan* my essays and see that I've got five clear main points. Only I hate planning. And I like side-tracks. You never know quite where they're going to take you. Side-tracks are like the little roads off the main road. The main road's all plain and straight whereas you never know where a side road is going to.

I suppose I'm side-tracking now.

Brent's rather taken over from the River Woman in our conversations. And she hasn't been around all week.

'D'you think she saw us watching her?' Gemma asked. 'Didn't you think she was a witch?'

'I was quite little then,' I said, even though it was only a few weeks ago. But I do feel much more grown up now. Since Brent, that is.

'Umm,' said Gemma. 'Well, I hope she didn't see us. I hope she isn't still lurking by all those graves plotting some horrible revenge on us.'

I felt too happy even to think of such things. 'I don't know who she is or what she's about,' I said, 'but I don't think she wants to harm us.'

I still didn't tell Gemma how seeing the River Woman bathing herself had made me think of river nymphs and Pan in *WITW*. There are some things I don't think Gemma would understand. I wonder if Brent would?

Chapter Ten

MY BROTHER *by Sam Haskins, Form 4N*

MY BROTHER'S NAME IS PETE. He has yellow hair and bluw eyes and a big big smile. He is 12 yers old.

My brother and me used to share a bedroom. I liked that. Pete had one bed and I had the othur. Sumtimes we wuld talk together in the nite. If my mum and dad were rowing Pete wuld tell me to pul the blanket over my head and not lissen. To go to sleep. Sumtimes he would come into my bed when I was feeling bad. He had a nice smell. Pete and me used to go to the park together and play football. Pete helped me on the climing frame because it is diffycult with my leg.

When our mum and dad were out Pete made us our tea. We had sausages and baked beens and lots of bred and marg. If Pete had any money we wuld go to the chippie and buy big porshuns of chips and eat them in frunt of the telly.

When Erasmus needed mending Pete would stitch him with a big needle. Pete is good at sewing. He sewed lots of patches onto his jeens. They look nice. Pete makes me laugh. He knows a lot of jokes.

My dad likes Pete because Pete is clever and good-looking and good at football. And Pete is strong. He doesn't walk odd like me and he doesn't need specs.

Pete says one day him and me will live together. Just the two of us. I wuld like that.

One day in school there was a fire alarm and Pete came to find me becos he knew I culdn't go fast down stairs.

My brother is the best brother. I wuld like to go to London becos that is where Pete is living now. He writes me letters. I like Pete's letters but I wuld like to see him.

I wish he was sharing my bedroom again
    It is not the same without Pete.

THE END

Sam, your brother sounds very nice.
You must miss him a lot.
I hope you see him again soon.

176 ELLIOTTS ROW, LONDON SE26

Hiya Bruv!
    Howya doing? Hope you like your new place. Have you got your own room? How is Erasmus? Bet he's as stinky as ever.
    Mum gave me your address. She and Dad are still not speaking. Sometimes on the phone I have to do the speaking for them. Like this.
    TO DAD: Dad, Mum says she needs some money.
    TO MUM: Mum, Dad says he'll send some when he can but he's got a lot of expenses just now.
    TO DAD: Mum says like going to the pub and taking out your fancy women. (I'm not sure what a fancy woman is are you? Sometimes Dad sees a woman called Elaine. But she's not at all fancy. She's very plain and a bit dull.)
    TO MUM: Dad says rent in London is very high and he's looking after me isn't he?
    TO MUM: Mum says you never did much looking after in the past.
    TO MUM: Dad says you weren't much of a mother either.
    That usually makes Mum cry and I don't know what to say then. So I say, 'See you soon Mum', though I don't know when that will be. Dad says he never wants to see her again.
    London is ENORMOUS. I have a new school. It's enormous too. Dad and me have been on the Big Eye. It's like a huge wheel at a fairground and you go round and round only very slowly and you can see all over London. I have

been lost on the tube twice. The tube is a train that goes underground. But there's lots of lights. When you come to London I will take you on the tube and we will go and see Buckingham Palace and the changing of the guard. And maybe go on a boat down the river.

You are well out of it at home, Sam and I hope they are looking after you well. Don't forget that we are going to live together, you and me. Soon as I'm old enough to get a job I will find somewhere for us to live.

Try and write me a letter.

If I can save up some money I will try and come and see you.

lots of love from your favourite brother Pete xxx
P.S. X for Erasmus, while holding my nose!

12 *February*, 2002   FLAT 15D, GOGARSTON ROAD, EDINBURGH, EH28

Dear Sam,

I hope you are well. It is very quiet here without you and Pete. Sometimes I have to put the telly on very loud to stop the quiet. The social worker says I need to rest for the new baby but it is hard when it's quiet like this. Like as if the world has stopped. Only I know it hasn't because there's still a leak in the kitchen ceiling and I can hear it dripping in the night. Put the red bucket under it and it's full in the morning. Because of upstairs. Them in the flat above just don't fix it, though I've asked and asked and even written a note.

No word from Dad. And no money. I am sorry he ever hit you, Sam.

I have given Pete your address so hope he will write to you. The social worker says I will have to go to court to get Pete back. I will do it when I am better. I am sickly a lot but I hope they will let you come home soon. I keep asking.

I am sorry not to have been to see you but there's been no money for the fare. Be a good boy where you are and don't be wetting the bed and making people cross.

your loving mum xxxxxxxxxxxxx

MEGAN'S HOUSE

Dear Pete,

I don't like it here. Please cum and see me. I have 50p pocket money. I am sending it to you.

There are two othur boys here. Raymond and now Brent. They are both nasty. And a girl called Anna. She is bossy.

I miss you loads.

love Sam xxxxx

MEGAN'S HOUSE

Dear Mum,

I am trying to be good. I don't get eunuf to eat here. I had a nice letter from Pete. Can you send somone to London to bring him home?

Please get well soon so I can come home. I will help you look after the new baby when it is born and I won't wet the bed any more or steal anything. I don't mind about the leak in the citchen. I will help you empty the bucket every morning.

There is a dog here called Toby. He is not very friendly.

lots and lots and lots and lots of love

Sam xxxxx

P.S. I am glad Dad has gone but not Pete.

Chapter Eleven

I DON'T THINK I'll ever understand boys. Gemma says that nursery rhyme about what girls and boys are made of is probably right. We're 'sugar and spice and all things nice' and they're 'frogs and snails and puppy dogs' tails'. Gemma said that because Mark Thornhill, who was so keen on her last week, is now chatting up Jane Leonard.

We had a good laugh about frogs and snails and puppy-dogs' tails being a perfect description of Raymond because he'd live in the river just like a frog if he could, and he's got a shell just like a snail. Only pops his head out now and again to say two words. Of course Toby-dog isn't exactly a puppy but he's got this question mark of a tail so when you see them together, skinny Raymond and questioning Toby-dog, it's like seeing an exclamation mark and a question mark side by side. We fell about laughing at that, Gemma and me.

Gemma comes to tea at our house now and I've been to hers. Her mother is terribly, terribly nice to me, so I know she feels sorry for me. I hate that. It brings out the worst in me, so I stopped saying 'please' and 'thank you' and I definitely did *not* smile at any of her little jokes.

When I was leaving I heard her say to Gemma, 'She's a rather sullen girl, isn't she?' Sullen! Me! Megan had to go and meet Gemma's mum before I was allowed to visit. It's one of the Social Work rules and so embarrassing.

I said, 'I suppose if I wanted to do a sleep-over at Gemma's, you'd have to check if Gemma's mum had a police record.'

And d'you know, Megan laughed and said, 'Well, possibly I might!' I ask you!

Anyway, I'm going to be nicer next time I'm invited to

Gemma's because I don't want to lose her as my best friend and I think Andrea Lloyd is trying to win her back again. She gave Gemma a special card last week, all flowery on the front and a message inside saying 'I miss you as my friend'.

I'm side-tracking again. This is about boys and how odd they are. Firstly there's Sam. All of a sudden he's stopped stuffing his mouth with everything and anything. In fact he seems to have stopped eating! Megan has to coax a mouthful of cereal down him in the morning and at supper-time he has a couple of spoonfuls of whatever it is and then pushes his plate aside. Goes off into a corner hugging Erasmus. Erasmus could do with another wash, but I'm not offering. Two days this week Sam wasn't well enough to go to school. Megan says she'll have to take Sam to the doctor. But what can the doctor do? It's obvious what's wrong with Sam. He's pining for his mum or that wonderful big brother of his. Or both.

Megan's so concerned with Sam she hasn't noticed what Raymond's been up to. But I have! While Sam isn't eating, Raymond seems to be stashing food in doggy-bags. Only they aren't for Toby-dog.

There's other things too. Raymond's school bag looked really fat the other day. Fat with blanket! One of the blankets from his bed. And at the bottom of the bag you could see the shape of what looked like tins. I also saw Raymond coming out of the chemist. What's he going to the chemist for?

'Raymond's up to something,' I said to Brent.

Brent's arm is better now which means he spends every spare hour playing his guitar. He's also added some green stripes to his hair. They don't really go with the pink ones.

'Uh-hu,' said Brent. He was trying out some new chords.

'He's taking things somewhere,' I said.

Brent began to look interested. 'What sort of things?' he asked.

'A blanket. Food. Oh and an old jersey Megan was going to give to Oxfam.'

'He's planning a flit,' said Brent. I could tell he thought this was rather exciting. Brent likes excitement. He likes really scary horror books.

'Don't you think we should tell Megan?' I asked.

'No,' said Brent. 'Maybe he's just making himself a den. Let's follow him.'

Really, I begin to think I might have a career as a private detective. Following people. There's lots of women detectives in television dramas these days. They're what Gemma calls 'feisty women'. I don't think I am 'feisty'. Not deep down. Deep down where there's divine discontent and hopes and fears and puzzles and wonders. Stuff like that.

Ever since I told Brent about my mum and her drinking and that, all sorts of pictures have been coming back into my head. It's like some of the clothes I've torn and hidden at the bottom of my drawer and then Megan fishes them out. They're sort of torn-up memories or like bits of a film. Only I know they're not part of a film. I know they really happened. One or two start off quite nice. Like when Mum got together with Jem at the beginning and we were going to be a happy family and Mum said we'd go on holiday and things and I could have a TV in my room. Then it sort of changes and Mum and Jem are throwing things at each other and I'm thinking there's going to be no furniture left if they carry on. And Mum shuts Jem out of the house and he breaks all the windows to get in again.

I'm trying to shove these memories back down again, but they don't seem to want to go back, back to the bottom of the drawer.

I don't think these things when I'm by the river, only when I'm on my own at night. Maybe the river washes them away. Anyway, I thought following Raymond might give me a chance to show Brent the river, to share it with him. So we did it on Sunday. Followed Raymond that is. Brent said we should just idle along as if we were going for a walk because after all Raymond didn't *own* the river, did he?

And I said, no, I thought maybe the River Woman

owned the river. So then I had to explain about the River Woman and how until this week she was always there and how Gemma and I had followed her to the abandoned cemetery and seen her bathing herself and how I thought she looked suddenly different, changed. As if the water had magic powers. Or she had.

'You mean she had nothing on?' said Brent.

'Not a stitch,' I said.

'Wow!' said Brent.

'She looked like . . . like a river nymph,' I said.

Brent didn't laugh. He just nodded as if he was quite used to river nymphs and water with magic powers and suddenly I was telling him all about *The Wind in the Willows* and how Ratty and Mole feel the presence of Pan and how that was how I'd felt and how it was a really good book and there was a character in it who was mad about cars. (I didn't tell him it was a toad.)

Brent said maybe he should read it and we held hands then and nearly lost sight of Raymond, struggling on with his knapsack and Toby-dog dancing ahead of him.

I was really glad Raymond wasn't heading in the direction of the abandoned cemetery because I never want to go there again, not even with Brent. But Raymond took the path that leads up the steps to the pizza place and onto the bridge. We had to hurry after him then because he was ducking and diving down alleys.

We hid round the corner when we saw him get near a block of flats and disappear down the steps to a basement flat.

'Perhaps it's a squat,' said Brent. 'Perhaps he's planning to break in and hide out there.'

Really, Brent may not have a *Wind in the Willows* sort of imagination, but he's certainly got one. I mean I don't think Raymond's bright enough to think of a squat.

'He's only ten!' I said.

'So,' said Brent. 'There's kids of Raymond's age living on the streets or down in the sewers in South America.'

'This isn't South America,' I said. 'Let's go and look.'

61

So we crept down and knelt under the window, just poking our heads up quickly, so we could see what was going on. The window was pretty dirty, with just some old rags acting as curtains but I saw enough.

'It's the River Woman!' I said. Because there she was, tucked up on a battered old sofa with Raymond's blue blanket over her and Toby-dog curled up at her feet and Raymond handing her a bowl of something. And they're smiling at each other. And talking! Raymond! Talking!

He had his back to us so it was the River Woman who spotted us, pointing a shaky finger at the window so that Raymond turned round. We bobbed down under the sill but Raymond rushed to the door and flung it open. He was holding a mug of something really hot in his hand and for a moment I thought he was going to throw it at us. Boiling oil over our heads or, at the least, boiling tea.

I've never seen Raymond looking so wild and angry. And kind of alive. All that closed-in look gone. Right out of his snail shell he was, scarlet in the face and really mad.

'You're not to tell! You're not to tell!' he screeched at us.

We backed away, Brent spreading wide his arms like someone facing a gun and making peace. 'No problem, man. No problem!' Brent said.

And then we walked home. Rather slowly.

'Some river nymph!' Brent said.

'Yeah!' I said, because I was feeling – well, somehow both silly and sad. All those stories I'd made up about the River Woman. Raymond hadn't said a word. He'd just made her his friend.

I saw Clara today and told her how I kept getting these memories and that they were like bad dreams.

Clara said sometimes things hurt so much you buried them deep down, but then they carried on hurting you inside, even if you didn't quite know it, so maybe it was better if you took them out and looked at them.

'As if they were photos,' I said, 'and not bad dreams.'

'Something like that,' said Clara.

So I told Clara about Mum's sister, Janie, and how she'd tried to stop Mum drinking. 'She was nice,' I said. 'And I think she cared about us. Both of us. But she kind of ran out of care.'

'It happens,' said Clara. 'But I didn't know you had an auntie.'

Actually I'd never thought of Janie as my auntie. I'd kind of blanked her out, along with some of the bad dream sort of memories. Not because she was bad, but because I missed her.

'I cried when Mum told her to go away and never come back,' I said. 'She used to cook us tea and I had a scarf she knitted for me. I kept it for ages and ages. Until I lost it. Like I lost her.'

'She sounds really nice,' Clara said.

'She didn't approve of Jem,' I said and I told Clara about how after a row with Mum, when they'd both been drinking, Jem hit her again and I tried to stop him. I could hear myself shrieking 'I wish you were dead!' Then he went off in the car and crashed it and he *was* dead.

'I'd wished it,' I said. 'And it happened.'

'Not because you'd wished it,' said Clara.

'Not because of magical thinking?'

'Definitely not,' said Clara. 'Because he was angry and drunk.'

I like Clara. She really listens. I mean I know she's paid to, but she listens as if she really cares. I think maybe she likes me. Surprise, surprise!

Chapter Twelve

I'M FEELING REALLY CONFUSED. Raymond's got all friendly (well, his version of 'friendly') and Brent's gone all strange and moody. A few weeks ago I'd have thought that just *looking* at the River Woman had put a spell on him. Now I think it's more likely that the snazzy red sports car that's been parked at the back of our house all week has put a spell on him.

As for Raymond, well I don't want to sound cynical, but Raymond knows that I know about his secret. And he knows I could tell Megan.

'Actually,' I said, 'I don't think Megan would mind if you told her about the River Woman . . .'

'Her name's Nerine,' said Raymond.

I was a bit gob-smacked by that. I mean I've thought of her for so long as 'the River Woman' that it had never occurred to me that she had a name, like everyone else, even if 'Nerine' was a rather odd name. Giving her a name made me feel she was losing the magic I thought she'd had.

'Whatever,' I said, 'I still don't think Megan would mind. I mean you're doing a good deed, aren't you, looking after the Riv . . . Nerine – while she's not well?'

Raymond went a bit red when I said that. 'It's not like that,' he said.

'What *is* it like then?' I asked.

We were sitting in Raymond's bedroom for the first time ever. Him on the bed, me on the floor. Raymond's got all these drawings stuck on his wall. River pictures of course. Drawings of the swans and the heron, the willows and the bridge. And one just of Nerine's face. They're good. I have to admit they're good.

'It's like we're friends,' said Raymond. 'She looks after

me and I look after her and we look after the river.'

I felt a bit cross at that. 'We look after the river' – as if they owned it, as if no one else looked after it, though actually no one else does, much. They throw things in it and leave their litter behind instead.

'She's beginning to sound like a foster carer,' I said. Yes, I *know* that wasn't very nice of me, but to tell you the truth I was somehow jealous of Raymond just then. He'd got such a special friend. I know I've got Gemma and maybe Brent (when he cheers up) but the River Woman – Nerine – well, even if she isn't magical, you feel she knows things other people don't.

'She's just a friend,' Raymond said again. 'She doesn't have any family.' I could tell he was about to clam up on me if I wasn't careful. 'And she doesn't like other people interfering,' he added, a bit fiercely. 'In fact she doesn't like people much at all.'

Just like Raymond, I thought, but I didn't say it. Instead, I said, 'OK. I won't tell Megan.'

'Or anyone else,' said Raymond.

'Or anyone else,' I said.

'What about Brent?'

'He's got other things on his mind. Anyway, I think he's anti-all-rules which means he's anti-Megan.'

Raymond just about managed to say 'thanks'. He looked quite worn out. I think that must have been the longest conversation he's had in his entire life!

'Could I come with you one day?' I asked. 'To meet Nerine. I could help look after the river.'

Raymond went all closed-up in his shell when I asked that. I suppose I know the feeling. He didn't want to share Nerine with anyone, just like I don't want to share Gemma with Andrea Lloyd.

'I'll think about it,' was as far as Raymond would go.

So that was that. It didn't exactly make me feel wanted, I can tell you. And then there was Brent acting all strange. I think maybe he thought he was only going to be here for a few days until things calmed down at home. I heard him shouting at his social worker, really shouting, and afterwards he just flung himself into his bedroom and wouldn't open the door even though I knocked and called and asked if he'd like a cup of coffee or anything.

I've seen him in the corridor at school, all hunched and surly-looking. And he shoulders his way out as if he didn't care who he pushed or shoved as long as he got out.

And here, in the house, he's like a moody caged animal. He goes up and down stairs half a dozen times an evening. He won't even settle to watch TV. He's up and down looking out of the window at the back. Looking at that natty little sports car that's been there all week. I can't imagine where its owner's gone. Maybe he or she is ill. Or away. I just know that car is getting to Brent.

I overheard Megan talking about Brent to Theresa the other day. Theresa's Megan's social worker. I was trying to tell Gemma how we each have a social worker and Gemma couldn't get the hang of it at all.

'Why couldn't you all share one?' Gemma wanted to know.

'Well,' I said, 'I might want to tell *mine* something I didn't want Megan to know and Megan might want to tell *hers* something she didn't want me to know.'

'I think we need one in our family,' Gemma said. 'My brother's always telling Mum things. Even when I've made him swear not to. He just can't keep his mouth shut.'

Theresa's not a bit like Clara. Clara's quite young and trendy. Theresa's fat and comfy. Oh and bright. I mean she always wears these really bright sweaters. I think she must knit them herself. And when she sits down she's got the sort of lap that looks as if it needs at least three babies in it.

I couldn't catch much of what Megan and Theresa were saying but there was talk of a psychologist and mood swings and Brent used to being out every night of the week.

'We've really cramped his style!' Megan said and they both laughed. But I didn't think it was very funny. I thought Brent might have divine discontent to absolute bursting point.

Several times I asked Brent if he'd like to talk and I felt really upset when he just said, 'What's the point?' because I thought we'd got close, him and me. I thought we'd be friends for ever and ever. Maybe more. I'd like to give him a great big hug but he's just blanked me out.

Yesterday I cut up my new M & S jersey. I haven't done that for ages.

Then today Brent actually decided to walk home from school with me.

'What's up with you, then?' he asked.

'What d'you think?' I snapped, because he was acting as if we'd been the best of mates all week.

'It's not you,' he said, 'it's just this place has been getting to me. Can't go anywhere, do anything without getting permission first. Anyone would think I was five, not fifteen.'

We walked round the back of the house like we always do because mostly Megan leaves the back door open.

Brent stopped beside the sports car. It was still there. Bright and shiny, almost, I thought, waiting for us.

And then Brent said, 'Fancy a ride?'

Chapter Thirteen

WELL, WHAT WOULD YOU DO? It was the greyest day you ever did see. And this car just sitting there. Bright red. Red as a post box on wheels. Unwanted. Unused. And Brent standing there looking ever so hunky and grinning at me now, saying 'Want a ride?'

And I *knew* I should say 'no', and I knew it was all wrong, but suddenly there was something like a burst of sunshine in my head, or like a firework going off with a thousands sparkling stars. And it wasn't just the car, of course. It was Brent and the thought of him and me. Together! Escaping! And being offered an adventure when you least expect it, when you think your life is going to go on and on in the same way. Always.

So I said, 'Well, maybe just round the block, eh?'

And the next thing Brent had this card out – I *think* it was a credit card and don't ask me how he got *that*! And it took *ages* for him to get the door open so that I'm standing there, first on one leg, then the other, thinking someone's going to spot us any minute and I'm remembering Brent saying 'Just show me a car I can't get in' and I think maybe this is it. Only suddenly he's done it and he's in the driving seat swinging open the other door for me and I'm in there and the seat's a deep, squidgy leather and it smells delicious!

Brent's fiddling with a piece of wire in the ignition and that takes another age and all the time I thinking *I could stop this now!* Only I don't. Then the engine's alive and so are we. Very, very alive.

'Belt up!' says Brent, so I do. And he does too and we're both laughing like mad and we're off.

It took more than round the block for Brent to get used

to the car. At first we did a kind of bucking bronco at every traffic light. Then we were going really smoothly. And fast.

Both of us had the windows wide open and my hair was blowing in the wind and all Brent's pink and green highlights shone and quivered and I was thinking all kinds of daft things like how it was in road movies when there was a car chase and about a picture I'd once seen called 'The Colorado Freeway.'

Brent started singing. He leant one elbow on the window and steered with one hand.

'The open road,' I shouted at the top of my voice. 'The poetry of motion! The *real* way to travel! The *only* way to travel! Here to-day – in next week tomorrow! O bliss! O poop-poop!'

'What are you going on about?' Brent yelled back.

'*Wind in the Willows* and Toad,' I yelled back, because I didn't care any more. 'Toad at his best and highest, Toad the terror, the traffic-queller, the Lord of the lone trail . . .'

And Brent roared with laughter. 'That's me!' he shouted, overtaking a very sedate Ford and swerving round a corner so fast that we seemed to be on just two wheels, 'The traffic-queller, the Lord of the lone trail . . .' And he tooted the horn really loud and we both shrieked 'Poop-poop!'

Actually there were lots of people leaving work now and no one could call this an open road. Just a very busy one. Brent had to do a lot of weaving in and out before we escaped the city traffic. Then we were heading for the motorway.

'The lone trail,' Brent repeated. 'That's what we want,' and he put his foot down hard.

And all of a sudden I was scared . . . I think it was the huge signpost pointing to Glasgow and Carlisle. I remembered how I'd said, 'Well, just round the block' and I remembered Jem too. And then I got this really sick feeling in my stomach.

Brent seemed to be going faster and faster and I didn't like to ask him to slow down. It would seem so wimpish and I wanted to feel wild and free and brave and grown up – only somehow I didn't. I just pulled my seat belt a little tighter.

'What d'you say to the seaside?' Brent shouted.

'I think maybe we should go back,' I said and my voice came out all small and childish.

'C'mon!' said Brent. 'We'll take it back. We can be back by eightish. I'll park it just where it was. Whoever owns it won't even miss it.'

'But Megan will miss *us*,' I said. And suddenly I had this really vivid picture of Megan in the kitchen. Megan looking out of the window for us. Megan maybe phoning Gemma. And I thought of my bedroom – which I've come to really like now – and Raymond and Nerine and even that pain in the neck, Sam. Out of the blue I felt, well, *homesick*.

'I think we should go back,' I repeated, only my voice was stronger now.

Brent looked really sulky at that. It made me think about how I'd heard Megan and Felicity talking about his mood swings. He played about with the steering wheel and kept changing the gears up and down so the car made a horrible noise like it was trying too hard.

'When *I* say,' he said. Then I felt really frightened.

Only it wasn't when he said, because we came to this sharp corner. It was one of those corners marked with zebra stripes that warn you to go carefully. Brent didn't. He had his foot flat down on the accelerator and he wrenched the wheel really hard and next thing I knew we were upside down in the ditch.

I was lying sideways with my face against the door and Brent was somehow sprawled across me. Even though my window was open, there was no way I could get out. Brent managed to undo his seat belt and heave his door open. He crawled out and somehow I found the catch on my belt and wriggled over the driver's seat and scrambled out beside him. I wasn't hurt. At least the bruises didn't come out until later. I just felt really strange and shaky. Brent was white as a sheet. It made his pink and green streaks look like lollipop colours on a ghost.

I sat down on the side of the road because I didn't feel my legs could hold me up and the next minute there seemed to be a lot of people about, only I couldn't quite focus. I heard a woman saying, 'Are you all right, dear?' And someone else saying, 'Just a couple of kids.'

Someone made me put my head between my knees. Brent was just pacing up and down, his breathing all funny. Sort of panting. Then we heard the police car siren, distant at first and then getting closer and closer, louder and louder until it was sounding in my head. For a minute I thought Brent was going to bolt. He looked all round him as if seeking a way out. But there wasn't one really, not with all those people about.

Then the police were there, two of them, asking our names and where we lived and how old we were, looking all round the car as if it was a dead body, which I suppose it was in a way.

'Been for a little ride, have you, sonny?' the older of the two said. Then he made Brent take a breath test. I was really shivering by then and Brent was still so panicky I didn't think he'd have enough breath for a breath test.

'He hasn't been drinking,' I said, but they took no notice.

And then it all became horribly unreal. The older policeman began a kind of chant. I know it sounds stupid but it made me think of the way people in church sometimes chant the Lord's Prayer because they know it by heart and they've said it often. Only this wasn't a prayer. It was more like an awful spell.

'I am detaining you,' the policeman chanted at Brent, 'under the terms of the Criminal Procedures of Scotland Act 1995, Section 14, on suspicion of stealing a car.'

Then he went back to his ordinary voice, opened the back door of the police car and said, 'In!' And in we both went, huddled together in the back seat in a way that might have been romantic, only it wasn't.

I took one last look at the sports car. It didn't look bright and shiny any more. It looked like I felt. Wrecked.

'Not a good idea to have your girl-friend with you,' the younger policeman said.

'I'm not his girl-friend' I said. I was quite surprised at myself, saying that. I mean a week ago I'd have been really pleased if someone called me Brent's girl-friend. 'We're both in foster care,' I said, 'together.'

'I see,' said the policeman, and he didn't say anything after that, though I could see him exchanging looks with the other policeman as if to say 'typical'!

It felt as if Brent and I had driven for miles and miles and hours and hours but that the journey to the police station was horribly short. It was dusk by now. Once we stopped at some traffic lights near a school and I saw a sign on the wall that said, THE SETTING DOWN OR UPLIFTING OF CHILDREN FROM THIS CAR PARK IS PROHIBITED. I read it and read it while the lights were on red and wished, wished like anything that I could be 'uplifted' from the police car and set down on a desert island somewhere.

The police station was in a really pretty square. All posh Georgian houses with a garden in the middle. The police station itself was what I call old-modern. Plain and tatty and with very rude graffiti on a side wall.

Once inside we were taken to the custody room and it was just like you see on telly – our names and addresses, then everything taken from us which was very embarrassing as apart from a half-eaten doughnut and my schoolbooks, I had my small blue rabbit that Janie gave me years and years ago and which I always keep with me.

Next, and worst of all, they separated us. The sergeant said something about waiting for a responsible adult, then they locked Brent up in a cell. At least they called it 'the detention room', but I caught a glimpse of it before they shut the door on him and they can call it what they like, but it was a cell. A concrete floor, no window and bare except for a bench. I couldn't believe it when I heard them lock the door as if Brent was some kind of dangerous criminal.

Then it was my turn. I think they called this room 'a holding room' but it was just another cell really. The only difference was that mine had a huge porthole in the ceiling. You'd need a ladder to reach it, or those iron things mountaineers knock in the side of mountains to help them climb up it. The walls were covered in writing. Names mostly. I wished I'd managed to keep a biro or something.

They left my door open. I almost wished they hadn't. It's hard to pick your nose or scratch your head with the door open and a sergeant coming to look at you every five minutes. It's hard to cry.

So I just sat on the bench and read all the names and thought, Megan's going to go ballistic and Brent's going to go to prison and probably I will too and please, please couldn't a genie appear in the porthole of the ceiling and *uplift* me! Now!

Chapter Fourteen

RESPONSIBLE ADULTS? If you ask me, there's not that many responsible adults and Brent's dad certainly isn't one of them.

We heard him, before we saw him. He was outside the police station, shouting at someone. And that someone was obviously Megan.

'What sort of a carer d'you call yourself, then? Eh? Eh?' he yelled. 'He's hardly been with you three weeks and he's off nicking cars. You're not fit to look after kids. Don't think you're going to hear the end of this, because you're not . . .'

Then another voice, Felicity's. 'Really, Mr Windward, this is quite unnecessary. Megan has looked after a great many children and . . .'

I didn't hear any more because the sergeant let Brent out of his cell and took us both through to another room. The interview room, I suppose, where all the 'responsible adults' were waiting for us. Not just Megan, Brent's dad and Felicity, but Clara too.

Megan and Clara looked really upset, but as soon as we walked in Brent's dad went bananas. He grabbed hold of Brent and began shaking him. Shaking and shouting at the same time and Brent went all loose and floppy like a puppet.

'What d'you think you were doing? Eh? Eh?' (Shake. Shake.) 'Haven't you caused your mother and me enough trouble already? Eh? Eh?' (Shake. Shake.)

'This is all your fault,' Brent's dad said, turning on Megan now. I think if the police hadn't been there, he might have shaken Megan too! His fists were clenched and his eyes were all poppy. He didn't look at all like what I expected a professor to look like. I thought professors looked sort of dusty and noble. And maybe remote, as if they were thinking very great thoughts and wouldn't notice if their boiled eggs weren't properly boiled. Brent's dad was big and at that moment very red-faced. He was wearing a thick black overcoat and the more he shouted the more he seemed to swell inside it.

There were two policemen in the room now and one of them said, 'Mr Windward, I must ask you to calm down and sit down.'

Rather nervously, Felicity tried patting his arm, as if he was an angry dog and she was afraid he might bite. But Brent's dad just shook her off.

'You can keep out of this,' he shouted. 'I turn to you for help and support and what happens? My son is in worse trouble than he was when he was at home. What sort of people do you use as foster carers, eh?'

'Mr Windward!' warned the policeman.

Then we all sat down, Brent's dad looking like one of those land mines that you've only got to touch with your toe to make it explode.

The interview room was better than the cells, but not much. It was bare except for a long table and hard school-type chairs. The windows had those bathroom glass panes that you can't see through. There was a tape machine fixed in the wall and one of the two policeman switched it on. Then the other began.

'Brent Windward, up to now you have been detained under the Criminal Procedures Act. I must warn you that you are now under arrest. Do you understand?'

'Yes,' said Brent, very low down, like his voice had sunk to his boots.

'You need not say anything but anything you do say will be taken down and used in evidence.'

Then came the charges. They seemed to go on and on for ever.

There was taking and driving away a vehicle,
Careless driving,
Driving without a licence,
Driving without insurance.

I must have been in shock because the list of charges all seemed to run together. It was as if I was hearing a foreign language when you can't work out when one word finishes and the next one begins. All I could register was Brent saying 'yes' and 'I did' and once or twice 'sorry'.

The table we were sitting at was covered in names just like the cell had been. Only these were carved in the wood. From where I was sitting most of them were upside down, but I read 'Rab', 'Chaz', 'Ali and Cathy', 'Muff'. Muff? Was there really someone called Muff? And did Rab and Chaz and Ali and Cathy and Muff all have knives? Were they left in this room for hours with nothing to do but carve their names and wait? And if you think you're about to disappear from the world and into prison, do you get this urgent desire to write your name just to remind yourself that you really do exist? That you've still got a life.

On the wall was a Crimestoppers poster. DEALT WITH! it said above a picture of someone's hands handcuffed at the wrists. That's what we're going to be, I thought, dealt with.

The sergeant had hardly got to the end of the charges when Brent's dad really did explode, turning on Megan and shaking his fist at her.

'This is all your fault. Negligence. That's what it is. Total and absolute . . .'

'Mr Windward. I'm as upset about this as you are,' said Megan, her voice very quiet. (We've let her down, I thought. We've really let her down.)

'Upset?' roared Brent's dad, pushing back his chair and standing over her, 'You? What d'you know about it? No son of mine is going to be left in the care of some woman who doesn't know what the hell she's doing.'

Brent hadn't said a word until then. Now he burst out with, 'I wish I *wasn't* a son of yours!'

I thought Brent was going to go berserk at that moment. He too flung back his chair. He had his head down as if he was going to charge at his father. As if he had horns on his head and was going to butt him to kingdom come. And

Brent's dad had his fists raised and then the sergeant took over.

'Mr Windward, if your conduct continues as it is you could be arrested for breach of the peace. I must ask you to desist.'

That seemed to stop Brent's dad in his tracks. He stood there, fat and furious, his hands still clenched into fists. Then he turned on his heel and banged out of the room and out of the police station.

We could hear him shouting as he went down the road. 'No son of mine . . . no son of mine . . .' then the slam of a car door, an engine roar and silence.

'And you, young lad,' said the sergeant. 'You better calm down too unless you want to be kept here overnight.'

Brent sank back in his seat.

'We didn't mean to go far,' I said. 'We only meant to go round the block.'

'I hope you realise that we could have charged you too,' said the sergeant. 'Being in a vehicle that you knew was stolen.'

I felt a wave of relief at that 'could have'. I think I'd been handcuffed and heartcuffed until then.

'You,' continued the sergeant to Brent, 'I hope you realise what a serious offence this is. You could have killed someone. Yourself. Young Anna, here. And you put everyone else on the road at risk.'

I think Brent had exhausted 'sorry'. But he looked it. Very.

'What happens now?' asked Megan.

'There'll be a report to the juvenile liaison officer and to the Children's Panel,' said the sergeant. 'And as Brent is nearly sixteen, the Procurator Fiscal has the option of taking this to court.'

'Court!' said Brent. And if his face had been white before, now it looked grey.

'For now you can take them both home,' said the sergeant.

So we collected all our things. I tucked my blue rabbit in my pocket. I wanted to hold it and nibble its ears like I used to do when I was little. But I just stroked it inside my pocket where no one could see. Felicity drove us home. Clara actually gave me a kiss and made my scarf all snug round my neck. Felicity just looked grim. She didn't come into the house. She just said, 'I'll be round to see you tomorrow, Brent.'

Megan had called in Mrs Bolton from down the road to look after Sam and Raymond. Soon as we walked in we could hear Sam crying. Megan ran up to see him. Then she packed us both off to bed with a hot-water bottle each.

'I'm disappointed,' was all she said. 'So disappointed.'

All night I dreamt of those cells at the police station. Over and over again the door kept clanging shut on Brent and it wasn't so much like the door of a cell, it was more like the door of a dungeon, a great big iron thing, studded with black nails, a sort of horror film dungeon. And Brent was down there in the dark of it, shouting for me. Only there was no way I could reach him. No way I could open that door.

CITY OF EDINBURGH COUNCIL
SOCIAL WORK DEPARTMENT
CHILDREN'S DIVISION
SHELDON HOUSE
QUEENSFERRY ROAD
EDINBURGH EH5

Mrs Janie Hamilton,   3 March, 2002
5 Claremont Park,
Leith,
Edinburgh EH6

Dear Mrs Hamilton,

I hope you won't mind my writing to you. I am the social worker for Anna Charlston who I believe to be your niece. I am not sure if you are aware that Anna has been in care for some time now. She has found it very difficult to talk about her past and it is only in recent weeks that she has begun to talk about you. This has led me to look back in our records for any family connections and to find your address.

Anna is a lovely girl. Bright and imaginative. She clearly has some good memories of times spent with you. I do appreciate that there was a difficult family situation with Anna's mother, who is now missing without trace, but I wonder if you would consider meeting Anna?

I haven't, of course, told Anna that I am writing to you and would understand if you would prefer not to be involved. But I hope you will consider a meeting which I would be very happy to arrange.

Yours sincerely,
Clara Gibbs

Chapter Fifteen

EVEN THOUGH I felt as if I'd hardly slept at all, I woke up early and there was this heavy cloud over my head. Or maybe *inside* my head. And then I was properly awake and remembering. I crept into Brent's room. He was still fast asleep, rolled up in his duvet like the chrysalis of a caterpillar that definitely doesn't want to turn into a butterfly. His clothes were all over the place. Jeans dropped on the floor. School shirts thrown over a chair. His blue and silver striped school tie, still knotted and hung on the wardrobe doorknob. I crept away.

When I got downstairs Megan said, 'You look awful, Anna!'

'She always looks awful,' said Sam.

'Shut it,' said Raymond.

That surprised me. Raymond taking my side. I gave him my toast.

'What's going to happen to Brent?' I asked Megan.

'Felicity will be here this afternoon,' she said. 'We may know more then. Are you sure you feel up to going to school?'

I didn't, but school seemed a better option than hanging about all morning waiting for Felicity. I remembered how grim she'd looked last night. Somehow I didn't think she'd bring good news.

When I got to school, Gemma said the same as Megan – 'You look awful, Anna.' And looking at myself in the cloakroom mirror, I did. Not pale and interesting as I'd like to look, but pale and sick, with great bags under my eyes. And it was definitely a bad hair day. My hair looked like my mind felt – as if it didn't know which way to go.

I told Gemma all about taking the car and crashing it and ending up at the police station. Actually I thought it made a rather good story so I couldn't help adding a few details to it, like the police chasing us and Brent and I heading for Gretna Green. I felt quite tragic by the time I'd finished.

But Gemma was really snotty about it.

'I think that was a totally silly thing to do,' she said. 'And if I were you I wouldn't have anything to do with a boy who does something like that.'

'I suppose you only like goody-goody sort of boys,' I said. 'Boys who do just what their mummies and daddies tell them to do. At least Brent has a sense of adventure.'

'There's a difference between having an adventure and breaking the law,' said Gemma, all righteous. And she tossed her red hair at me (she must have washed it that morning, she tossed it with such a flourish) and went off with Andrea Lloyd.

I felt even worse then. Of course I do *know* it was wrong. But there was a moment when it felt wonderfully free and exciting. When we sped along shouting 'Poop! Poop!' it was as if we'd escaped out of our lives, out of time.

I've had that feeling before. It was once when Janie took me to the seaside and we spent all day on the beach and, late in the afternoon, Janie fell asleep on the rug and when she woke up she looked at her watch and said, 'Goodness, I've lost all track of time.' But really it was as if time had lost track of us. Somehow I think that's what divine discontent's about. Feeling trapped in time, inside your own life, and knowing there's all these centuries before you and after you that you'll never get into. Time's like space. Vast. And each of us get such a tiny portion.

I don't suppose I could tell any of *that* to the police. And it's no excuse for what we did. But I think if people understood, people like Gemma, how *unfree* Brent often felt, then they might understand a bit more.

Gemma sat with Andrea all morning and I was left with Myra Herbert who's really snidey. 'What's happened to you this morning?' she asked, looking at my hair. 'Been through a hedge backwards?'

'It's the latest wild look,' I said.

'Oh yes,' she said. 'The I-forgot-to-comb-it look.'

No one ever gets the last word with Myra.

It was double English this morning. Mrs Nobes has been getting us to write pen portraits of relatives. A pen portrait is like a picture in words. We're to match them in art class and then there's to be a display at the end of term.

'I suppose you haven't got any relatives, have you?' said Myra, because she knows about me being in care – or 'looked after' as Clara calls it.

'As it happens, I have,' I said. 'I've got an Auntie Janie.' It came out, just like that, without me even thinking about it first. It was as if Janie had just sent me a message saying, 'Here I am'. So I wrote about her.

And here's something really strange. Writing about Janie made me remember all sorts of things about her that I thought I'd forgotten. I mean I remember how Mum said Janie and I had the same sort of imagination, and the same nose! (A snub!) I don't know why, but it really pleased me remembering that. I felt like those archaeologists must feel when they dig up something from years and years ago.

I remembered, too, how when Mum and Janie were still speaking, we all used to go to see a film and on the way home we'd link arms and dance down the road. Sometimes we'd stop for fish and chips. Janie always paid. We were always broke. That was all before Jem was living with us and before the drinking got really bad.

I was still writing about Janie when the bell went. Myra had finished her pen portrait halfway through period two. She was writing about her Uncle Rex.

'I suppose you can't help being slow when you have to make it up,' she said.

'I didn't have to make it up,' I said. 'I *do* have an Aunt Janie. I expect you were quick because your Uncle Rex is so dull there's not much to say about him.'

'Two pages,' said Myra, waving them at me. 'Some of

us just have quick brains.' She'd got the last word again.

I didn't think about Brent at all while I was writing about Janie. But the rest of the day just dragged. At least Gemma and I made friends again. She was waiting for me when school finished. We didn't talk about Brent or the car or the police. It was like there was this big invisible statue between us and we were walking all round it, pretending it wasn't there.

But at least when Gemma went off up her road. she shouted back at me – 'Hope it's all OK' – which was generous of her considering what she *really* thought.

I ran all the way home. Megan was in the kitchen. So were Raymond and Sam. Scoffing cake.

'Brent?' I panted.

'In his bedroom,' said Megan.

'But what did Felicity say?'

'Brent's to go to the Young People's Unit until we know whether there's to be a Children's Hearing or if he'll have to go to Court.'

'The Children's Home!' I cried. 'But why? Why can't he stay here?'

'Social Services think you two are better apart. And you know, Anna, Brent only came here as an emergency. He wouldn't have stayed long anyway.'

'They'll send him to prison and I'll never see him again,' I said and burst into tears.

Megan put her arms round me. 'I very much doubt it,' she said. 'He may get off with a warning as it's a first offence. Or perhaps probation.'

'You're just trying to comfort me,' I shouted and I pulled away from Megan and went dashing up the stairs to Brent's room.

I didn't bother to knock. I just barged in. Brent was back in the chrysalis of his duvet.

'Go away!' he said.

Chapter Sixteen

THERE WAS a terrible mood in the house the next morning. I almost wished it was a school day and not the weekend. Brent came down for breakfast and wouldn't speak to anyone. Just sat slouched over his cornflakes. I think his eyes were what they call 'smouldering'.

Megan and Raymond were both really uptight too. It's not only Brent who's worrying Megan. Raymond's got his Review on Monday. I know about Reviews and it's hard not to worry about them. Even though the Children's Panel are often really nice you've got this feeling that they can decide your future. It's like the way grown-ups sometimes say 'We know what's best for you' and maybe they do and maybe they don't. Also it's hard to say what you want when often you only know what you *don't* want.

As for Sam – Sam seems away with the fairies these days. There's a really blank look in his eyes. Some days I think he looks like a little old man. It's as if he's given up hope. I think he's even given up eating!

So, there we all were. One big, unhappy family. Brent went back to his room straight after breakfast. I could hear him playing something really gloomy on his guitar. Great angry chords. I think I mean *discords*. Anyway, the sort of sounds that set your teeth on edge and make you wish for ear-plugs. Megan winced and shut herself in the kitchen with the dishes.

'We could take Toby-dog for a walk,' Raymond said. 'Along the river.' Raymond was sitting on the floor drawing a picture of the heron. He's always drawing these days. It was a good heron. He'd got the way the heron uses its legs as if they were stilts, lifting each one very carefully. Raymond's heron was poised on one leg.

I knew Raymond's suggestion of a walk was his way of

saying he was sorry about the stolen car and everything. I felt more like crawling back into bed than going for a walk, but then an offer to go along the river with Raymond could well be a once-in-a-lifetime opportunity. It could well be like being invited to Buckingham Palace and saying 'Ask me some other time.' So I said, 'Well, yes, OK. Thanks.'

Megan thought it was a good idea too. 'Take your mind off things,' she said and made us both wrap up warm with scarves and woolly hats. I thought that if Brent's dad could see us now, he'd *know* how good Megan is at looking after people. Raymond insisted on taking his rucksack which looked really full and heavy.

'Do you need that?' Megan asked, prodding it. But Toby-dog was making such a fuss, jumping up and down and barking like he does when he knows there's a walk on offer, that we were out of the house before Raymond could answer.

'I thought you might like to meet Nerine,' Raymond said shyly when we were outside, Toby-dog tugging us along.

There and then I gave Raymond a hug.

'Geroff!' he said. 'Nerine's better now. At least better enough to be back on the river.'

'I still don't know why you don't tell Megan about the Riv . . . about Nerine?' I said. 'I'm sure she'd understand. She might even help. Nerine looks as if she could do with some help. I mean she hasn't any money, has she? There was hardly any furniture in her room and her clothes are all tatty.'

'She doesn't want charity,' said Raymond. 'You have to understand. She's a bit like the heron.'

Actually we saw the heron as we walked towards the bridge, Toby-dog off the lead now and bouncing ahead of us, tail curled into a question mark. The heron was on the other side of the river, close to the wall, picking its way along on its tall, thin legs, sharp-eyed and slow. I thought it was a strong, solitary and mysterious creature. Maybe that's what Raymond meant when he said Nerine was like the heron.

Nerine was building another bonfire when we found her. She'd dragged all sorts of things out of the river. She'd piled up anything burnable – broken branches, boxes, dried-up reeds, old newspapers – and was just getting ready to light it.

She smiled when she saw Raymond. It was the first time I'd seen her smile and it made her look much younger, almost like she did that time Gemma and I had watched her bathing. But the smile faded when she saw me. I hung back a bit. Not that I can hide behind Raymond because I'm taller than he is, but somehow it seemed polite. I felt like being polite. Despite her old clothes and her hair with bits of twigs in it, there was something grand about Nerine. I reckoned she had what Brent's dad tried to pretend he had – a kind of inside pride.

Raymond said. 'I've brought my friend Anna to meet you because she's been wanting to for a long time and I've brought you some bread and cheese, oh and there's a bit of apple crumble I put in a tub and a packet of tea.' He said it all in one breath. An absolutely *major* speech for Raymond! (So *that's* what the rucksack was about.)

Nerine straightened up, put her hands on her hips and looked at me very steadily for what felt like ages. Actually, it felt as if she wasn't looking so much *at* me, but *inside* me. Then she turned back to her bonfire and began adding more sticks.

'You were watching me,' she said. She wasn't looking at me any more. I thought she probably didn't need to. She'd had me sussed in the first long look.

'You and that other girl,' she said. 'Watching me when I was private.'

'I'm sorry,' I said. 'We shouldn't have done that.'

'S'pose you thought I was a witch,' she said. 'People do, who don't know any better.'

'Actually,' I said. 'I thought you were a river nymph or maybe a swan maid because when you were – you know – in the river . . .'

'In me birthday suit . . .' she said.

86

'Yes, in your birthday suit,' I repeated, wishing I hadn't begun this, 'well, you looked, you looked . . . (this was getting worse) well, beautiful,' I finished.

Nerine stopped adding sticks to the bonfire, put her hands back on her hips and laughed. At least I think it was a laugh. It sounded half like a cackle and half like the noise seagulls make when they're rushing off somewhere.

'Listen to the child!' she said. 'River nymph! Swan maid! Beautiful! Raymond, your friend Anna's a funny one. Got a mind that runs away with itself. Runs fast and slow, like the river. Full of stories. That's like the river, too. Full of stories. Once-upon-time stories about mills and dams and bridges. About foxes and hares, salmon and magpies.'

(About Ratty and Mole and Badger and Toad, I thought.)

'I don't suppose your friend's much good at practical things, is she?' said Nerine, just as I'd kind of drifted off into *Wind in the Willows* land.

'Oh but I am,' I said. 'I can cook scrambled eggs and I can read a map a bit and sometimes I help in the garden and . . .'

'All right,' she said. 'I don't need a list. You need steadying, you do, with your flights of fancy. You can both help with this bonfire.'

We didn't need asking twice. We gathered up all the wood we could find and piled it on top. I was dying to see it lit. I wished Raymond had brought something sensible like potatoes we could have roasted in the embers as I think gypsies do. Or did.

And the bonfire was great when it got going. Nerine wouldn't let us get too close, but even standing back a bit it was warm. Lovely and warm and alive.

I felt Nerine had decided I was OK – even if I did need what she called 'steadying' – so I said, 'Why d'you do this, all this looking after the river?'

'Cleaning and burning,' she said. 'You've got to save the past and keep things clean for the future.'

I looked about me then and thought about how the river began, miles away in the hills, so maybe the hills were the past and the sea, where the river rushes to, is the future. Mrs Nobes says I get history and geography muddled up and that a faraway *place* isn't at all the same as a faraway *time*. Only they seem somehow similar to me. Maybe it's because my past, my past with my mum, seems far away in place *and* time.

'Raymond's my good friend,' Nerine said. 'Him and me. We're kin.'

'Kin?'

'Alike,' she said. 'Two of a kind. Peas of a pod.'

'I suppose you are,' I said, feeling a bit left out.

'You're the fiery one,' she said, tossing a few more sticks on the bonfire so that it sent out dozens of sparks that Toby-dog tried to chase, only they faded before he reached any.

'You'll keep us going,' she said. 'Stories. That's what we live on. Even daft ones like yours.'

I didn't have a clue what she was talking about. I wasn't even sure if she was paying me a compliment or ticking me off.

'You two had better be on your way or you'll get into trouble,' she said. 'Leave the food for me, Raymond. It'll last me, that.'

Raymond took the bread, cheese, apple crumble and packet of tea out of his rucksack. He'd packed them in a carrier bag. He left them high up on the bank for her.

'You're a good lad,' she said. And to me, 'No more watching me when I'm private.'

'Never,' I said. 'I'll never do that again.'

We began to walk away, Raymond, Toby-dog and me. Nerine stood letting the bonfire die down and watching the river.

'Troubled,' I heard her say, 'the river is troubled.'

I couldn't think why the river was troubled. I thought probably Nerine knew all its moods and had decided that this one was troubled. I thought that even if she *wasn't* a witch or a river nymph or a swan maid, even if she was just an ordinary old woman, she was also extra-ordinary.

'It's a funny thing,' said Megan, when we got home, 'but I'm sure I had another loaf of bread and that there was some apple crumble left.' And she gave what I can only call a very pointed look at Raymond's now empty rucksack.

Megan took Brent his lunch on a tray.

'Just leave him be for a while, Anna,' she said. 'He's got things to think about.' But she let me take him a cup of coffee.

'Can I come in?' I asked.

'Please yourself,' said Brent. He was lying on his bed reading a magazine.

'You won't get sent to prison,' I said. (I hadn't meant to start like that, but Brent wasn't making conversation easy.)

'Thanks a bundle,' he said.

'And it might not be too bad at the children's home,' I burbled on, 'and I expect your dad will calm down. Probably Felicity will be able to sort things out and you'll go home again. They'll be missing you and you'll be missing them and . . .'

'Oh blah de blah de blah!' said Brent and he put his headphones and Walkman on.

'You might try to remember I'm your friend,' I said and slammed out.

I felt bad about that afterwards, so I spent all afternoon making him a good luck card. I drew a picture of us having coffee at that café in town on the day we'd had such a good time together. And I put a guitar in one corner and a big bunch of flowers in the other. Inside I wrote:

> Wherever you are
> Near or far
> Wherever you go,
> I want you to know
> I'll be your friend
> Time without end

I was really pleased with it. It's the first time I've written a poem. Maybe I won't be an actress after all. I'll be a poet instead. I slid the card under Brent's door.

After that I didn't know what to do with myself so I found this book Megan has about people in myths and I looked up 'Nerine'. It said, *a daughter of Nereus.* And when I looked up Nereus it said he was *the wise and unerring old man of the sea.*

I asked Megan what 'unerring' meant and she said it meant always getting things right.

In the evening Brent came down to watch telly. He plumped himself beside me on the sofa and dug me in the ribs with his elbow.

'Thanks for the card,' he said.

'It's OK,' I said. The knot which had been in my tummy all day suddenly undid itself.

'Want to help me pack tomorrow?' he asked.

I wanted to say, 'But I don't want you to go!' Instead I just said 'OK.'

So that's what we did on Sunday and it was sad, sad, sad. There wasn't a lot to pack really and Brent's method was just to throw everything in his bag. I took all his clothes out again and folded them neatly like I thought Megan would have done. Then we zipped up the bag and just sat there looking at each other.

'Burning and cleaning,' I said.

'What?'

'It's what the River Woman says. You've got to save the past and keep things clean for the future.'

I suppose I was thinking that I wanted to 'save' our friendship and make it last on and on into the future. But Brent just said, 'I don't think I want to save my past. I'd rather make a bonfire of it.'

'But we'll still meet,' I said. 'Whatever happens?' Somehow that turned into a question.

'Maybe,' he said.

'No, not *maybe*,' I said. 'For sure.'

'Anna! Anna! Anna!' said Brent. And then he kissed me! I really like that sentence. I wish I could make it grow.

I wish I could make it a big long kiss on the lips. Only it wasn't. It was just a little kiss. On my nose! I might never blow it again.

When I was in bed I began thinking about Nereus, the old man of the sea. I wish I could be 'wise and unerring'. And I remembered a river poem Mrs Nobes read to us about the river really being

> *her Mighty Majesty the sea,*
> *Travelling among the villages incognito.*

I had to ask Mrs Nobes what 'incognito' meant and she said it meant 'in disguise'. So maybe Nerine's like that too. Maybe she really *is* the daughter of Nereus, only in disguise. I bet she'd tell me that was a daft story.

I wish I could make things right for Brent. For Brent, me and the river.

All of us troubled.

Chapter Seventeen

I T WAS *Raymond's Review* yesterday. I've been trying not to show him that I was worried about it. 'It's just a bit of a check-up,' I told him, 'to see you're doing all right. And you are, aren't you?'

'Suppose,' Raymond said. There's no kidding Raymond really. He's sharp.

I had three worries. Top of the list was Miss Holland who would certainly be asked to attend the Review. There'd been the truanting episode and although Miss H had given Raymond a 'B' for his river essay, I knew she didn't like him. On his last report she'd written, 'Although Raymond's work has improved a little this term, he still fails to participate in class discussions. Mostly his mind seems to be elsewhere and he is generally unresponsive.'

Then there was Raymond's mum and the delightful Stan. Would they turn up? And if they did, what would they say? I felt ninety-nine per cent certain they wouldn't want Raymond home, but would they be willing for him to stay with me? Dawn Eccles is unpredictable. Whenever she does manage to turn up for a meeting she looks at me with accusing eyes. I suspect she'll do whatever Stan suggests – she's under his thumb.

And lastly there's the Children's Panel itself. There's always three people on the Panel and they're meant to consider what's in the best interest of a child – his needs more than his deeds. But that doesn't mean they always come up with the decision you want.

I was glad, when we got there, that one of the Panel was Mrs Powell who we saw last time. 'Nice to see you both again,' she said when we came in. She was the Panel chairman and introduced us to the other two – Mrs Jordan and Mr Fellowes. All three sat behind a long table full of files and notepads. And there was the Reporter at the far end of the table, taking notes. It always feels a bit like having an interview for a job. Only this is an interview for a life, a child's life. Raymond's life.

Our chairs were ranged in front of the table in a semicircle. They try to make it as cosy as possible – there were children's drawings on the wall and a toy farm on a window ledge – but it isn't. I could tell Raymond had done what he always does when he's troubled. Withdrawn into himself. Closed up.

Alison, Raymond's social worker, and Miss Holland were already there. I knew Alison would speak in favour of Raymond staying with me. It was Miss Holland I feared. She gave us a nod. Not a smile, a nod. I knew she wasn't on our side from that nod.

Mrs Powell looked at her watch. 'We're just waiting for Mrs Eccles,' she said, 'then we can begin.'

We heard Raymond's mum and Stan coming along the corridor. Arguing.

'You won't go changing your mind,' I heard Stan say.

'It isn't easy for me,' Dawn replied.

'Easier without him,' said Stan.

Stan gave Raymond a wink as he came in and then didn't look at him again. He sat slumped in his chair, his arms folded. Dawn gave Raymond a quick kiss and then looked anxiously at Stan in case she'd done the wrong thing.

I thought, this isn't going to go well.

Alison gave the first report. Said she was very pleased with the way Raymond had settled in and she thought he'd become more outgoing in recent weeks. Then Mrs Powell asked me if Raymond got on well with the other children in the house? That was difficult. It's only recently that Raymond and Anna seem to have made friends. Before that Raymond's been a loner. I told them all the good things I could think of about Raymond. What I wanted to say was, 'Look, I love Raymond and I think he's beginning to love me.' But it didn't seem the right time to say it.

Mr Fellowes turned to Dawn and Stan. 'I understand, from the social worker's report, that you feel unable to have Raymond at home and think he would be best in permanent foster care. Is that correct?'

'We can't have him,' said Stan before Dawn could say a word. 'Dawn here can't cope with him always rowing with Mary. Fighting. Being nasty. Anyway, she's expecting again . . .'

'Mrs Eccles?'

Dawn looked as if she was being torn apart. 'Well, of course I'd like to have Raymond home if I thought we could manage . . .'

'But we can't,' said Stan. He patted Dawn's knee. 'She has a mother's feelings of course. But she can't cope, can you, dear?'

'No,' said Dawn and I could see that she was crying.

And Raymond? How can you tell what's going on in a child's heart at such a moment? His face looked frozen over.

'Course we'll see him regular,' said Dawn, wiping her eyes.

Mrs Jordan asked Raymond if he would be happy staying with me and if he'd like to carry on doing so.

'Suppose,' said Raymond, head down, tight in his shell.

'We need to feel a little more certain than that,' said Mrs Jordan. She had friendly eyes, Mrs Jordan. 'I always clam up when people ask me how I'm feeling,' she said. 'You probably feel the same.'

Raymond gave a very small smile. 'So tell us,' continued Mrs Jordan. 'Would you be happy if we said you were to carry on living with Megan? If that was to be a permanent arrangement?'

'Yes,' said Raymond, loud and clear now. 'I like it there.'

And then Miss Holland had her go. She talked about Raymond playing truant, about him not making friends at school, not taking part in anything. 'Being remote and sullen' is how she described it.

The Panel all began to look very solemn and concerned and I badly wanted to hold Raymond's hand and tell them that Miss Holland just didn't have a clue about Raymond when the door burst open and the strangest woman you ever did see came in.

She was wearing an ancient flowery hat, a long silk scarf, what looked like several rather threadbare coats one on top of the other and wellies.

A frantic receptionist ran in behind her. 'I'm sorry, this lady burst in!' said the receptionist, scarlet with embarrassment. 'She said she had something very important to say.'

'That I have,' said this apparition.

I turned to Raymond and saw he was grinning all over his face.

'Does this lady have legal rights to attend this Review?' asked Mrs Powell.

'Legal rights? I got love rights,' she answered.

The Panel exchanged looks. Mrs Powell consulted the Reporter. The Reporter nodded. 'Well then, you'd better sit down,' said Mrs Jordan and she pulled up an extra chair. 'And you are . . . ?'

'Nerine,' Raymond answered for her.

'That's right,' she said; ignoring the chair. 'And Raymond here's my friend. Helps me with the river. Helps me when I'm poorly.'

'The river?' prompted Mrs Powell.

'Looking after it,' said Nerine. 'Keeping it clean. Keeping it healthy. Raymond's the best boy there is. My friend.'

'I know Raymond's very fond of the river,' I put in.

'He did quite a good essay about it,' Miss Holland admitted reluctantly.

'And when you were poorly,' Mrs Jordan continued, 'you said Raymond helped you?'

'Brought me food. Made me tea. Looked after me,' said Nerine. 'And he does these pictures.'

(My pie, I was thinking! That piece of cheese! That

95

blanket that vanished. Now I knew where they'd gone.)

From out of her carrier bag, Nerine produced a whole sheaf of drawings. There were the swans with their new cygnet. The heron. The willow trees. The bridge. The pigeons roosting in their holes in the wall. The drawings were passed over to the Panel.

Dawn and Stan just sat there with their mouths open.

'That's all I got to say,' said Nerine, bashing her hat down firmly on her head so that bits of straw fell out of it. 'Raymond's a good boy. He's a river boy. Needs to stay where he is.'

'We're most grateful to you,' said Mrs Jordan, but Nerine had already taken the drawings out of her hands and was off.

'Well,' said Mrs Powell, 'I think we've heard all we need to know. My opinion is that the best thing for you, Raymond, is that you continue to stay with Megan and we'll review the situation in another year. Mr Fellowes?'

'I agree,' said Mr Fellowes. 'And perhaps improve a little on things at school? I'm sure Miss Holland here has been pleased to see such a display of talent in your art work.'

Miss Holland managed a small smile.

'I agree too,' said Mrs Jordan.

It was over. At least apart from the goodbyes.

I went and looked in a shop window while Raymond said goodbye to his mum. I could see their reflections. They hugged. I could see Raymond clinging on to her, his arms round her neck. Then Stan pulled her away. 'Come and see you soon,' Dawn called.

For a moment Raymond just stood there and I thought I'd never seen a child look so hurt and lonely.

'Come on,' I said, 'I want to hear all about Nerine and the river and what the two of you have been doing together.' And I put my arm round him and gave him a kiss.

Raymond said, 'You know you can't kiss it better.'

'I know I can't,' I said. 'I can't change the past and nor can you. We can just try for a better future.'

*Raymond heaved a big sigh, took my hand and said,
'Let's go home!'*

'Let's,' I said.

*I know Raymond will grieve for his mum, but I think –
I hope – he'll be happy here. I hope he'll be able to stay
with me for a long time. More than this year. More than
next. Sometimes, when he's hidden inside himself he
reminds me of a bulb you plant deep in the soil in autumn
and then very slowly, come spring, you begin to see a small
green shoot. So I say to myself, Raymond will grow sturdy
and strong and his talents will flower.*

*I wish I could say the same about Brent and Sam. Brent
left yesterday. (Talk about everything happening at once!)
I don't feel he's had a proper chance here. I hope he doesn't
get taken to court and somehow I have the feeling that
being sent to the children's home will make him angrier
than he is already.*

*As for Sam, at the moment he's like a little zombie and
nothing seems to cheer him up. Not even the letters from
his brother.*

*And Anna? How is she going to react to Brent leaving?
She was in tears when Felicity came to collect him and
Anna doesn't cry easily. I wonder, too, how long it's going
to take her to come to terms with her real past, instead of
the fantasy one which, of course, is much nicer!*

*   *

From: janie hamilton <j.hamilton@gateway.com>
To: <gibbs.clara@edin.cit.socserve.com>
Sent: 30 March 2002 8.22

Yes! Yes! Yes! Letter to follow.

Chapter Eighteen

JUST WHEN I thought nothing good would ever happen again, something amazing has happened. Clara has found Janie!

Clara turned up on Wednesday afternoon, which is not her usual day. She was looking all bright and cheery, wearing a scarlet scarf and lipstick to match. Sometimes it seems quite insensitive of people to look happy when you're feeling miserable, so I said to Clara, 'If you've come to talk about Brent, I don't want to know.'

Actually, I *did* want to know. I wanted to know why, since I've written to Brent every day without fail, I haven't had one single reply. And I wanted to know how you can tell if your heart is broken and if anyone has died of a broken heart apart from Romeo and Juliet and in my opinion they died by mistake.

But Clara said, 'I haven't come to talk about Brent. I've got some news for you. Let's go and sit down.'

And then I went hot and cold. She's come to tell me I've got to go to another foster home, I thought. All that trouble with the car and the police, it won't just be Brent who gets punished.

Clara must have seen the look on my face because she laughed and said, 'It's good news, Anna!'

So then Clara tossed off her coat and we sat side by side on the sofa and Clara dug about in that bag of hers that has everything but the kitchen sink in it, until she pulled out a letter. Then she held my hand and said, 'I've found your Aunt Janie.'

I must have gone white, because Clara said, 'Shall I get you some water?'

And I swallowed hard and said, no, I was all right. I mean I was STUNNED!

'But where? How?' I don't know why, but I suddenly felt frightened. I've thought a lot about Janie recently and sometimes I've thought that one day, when I'm grown up, I'll be walking along the street in somewhere like San Francisco and suddenly she'll be there. We'll both recognise each other. We'll stop and she'll say, 'Anna?' and I'll say, 'Janie?' and we'll fall into each other's arms.

There's another version of this story. I'm back with my mum and she's sober now and we've got a nice ground floor flat with a garden and one day who should walk up the garden path but Janie. Then it's Mum and Janie who fall into each other's arms and I'm just in the background, but smiling and smiling and smiling.

Anyway, that's all very different from learning that *the real Auntie Janie* has been found.

'She's living in Leith,' said Clara.

'But that's just down the road,' I said and burst into tears.

'Oh dear,' said Clara, fishing a load of tissues out of her bag, 'I thought you'd be really pleased.'

'I am! I am!' I sobbed. 'It's just not like *This Is Your Life*!'

'What on earth d'you mean?'

'That TV programme where they bring long lost relatives from the end of the world. I mean she's been living so near all this time and I didn't know and she didn't know and I've missed her and missed her and missed her!'

'Maybe you're crying for all you've missed and lost,' said Clara. 'Not just Janie.'

'Maybe,' I said. I was down to snivels and nose blowing now. 'But I could have found her in the phone book . . . if I'd looked. How did *you* find her?'

'Well,' said Clara, 'it's only recently you've begun talking about Janie . . .'

'I'd sort of blanked her out,' I said.

'Yes. I was surprised when you began talking about her. And when you did, I thought I'd just look back in our records to see if her name was there. To see what *family* was there really. There were no grandparents listed. And your mum . . .'

'Missing,' I said.

Clara gave me a quick hug. 'Yes, missing. Father . . .'

'Unknown,' I said. 'Brilliant family tree, don't you think?'

'And then there was a J. Charlston, and an address. Only she wasn't there any more. But the people who were there said they thought she'd married. So then I had to look at the records for marriages and that's how I found her. Her name's Hamilton now. That's why you wouldn't have found her in the phone book, even if you had looked.'

Clara was still holding the letter in her hand. 'That's from her, isn't it?' I said.

'Here,' said Clara, giving it to me. 'It's a nice letter. She wants to meet you.'

For a moment I just held the envelope, stroking it with my finger, gently. A letter from *my* aunt, my very own aunt.

'Someone I belong to,' I said.

'Take it easy, Anna,' said Clara. 'It may not mean more than a meeting – maybe just once. Maybe just now and again.'

Then I opened the envelope. I read Clara's letter to Janie first. Then I read Janie's e-mail. Then I read this:

5 CLAREMONT PARK, LEITH, EDINBURGH EH6

2nd April, 2002

Dear Clara Gibbs,

I was delighted to receive your letter. I have very fond memories of Anna. I had no idea that she was no longer with her mother. As you probably know, my sister and I quarrelled many years ago and completely lost touch. I always presumed that Anna was with her and hoped, one day, that I might hear from her.

I would very much like to meet her. It might be a good

idea if you and I met first so that I could catch up a little
on Anna's life.

I look forward to hearing from you,
yours sincerely,
Jane Hamilton

'You're going to see her!' I said.
'Friday,' said Clara with a grin.

Chapter Nineteen

I THINK I've forgotten how to talk. And there's so much I want to say – about Janie. About Clara going to see Janie, about Janie coming to see me, about me going to see Janie. That last one hasn't happened yet.

Maybe it's not so much that I've forgotten how to talk, but that I don't know who to talk *to*. There's Megan and Clara, of course and I know they're both very understanding, but I'm not certain they understand JOY. I'm not certain anyone over sixteen understands joy and how strong it is and, at the same time, really delicate.

From the moment Clara told me she'd found Janie, I've felt as if there's a spring bulb growing inside of me, pushing up and up towards the light. Something like a tulip that will suddenly open its lovely red petals. That's the strong joy bit. And then I've felt that I've got to look after that, like the earth looks after the bulb, keeps it warm and snug and secret until it's ready. That's the delicate bit. Maybe that's what's making it difficult to talk.

It's as if finding Janie, finding someone of my own family, is so wonderful and precious that I'm scared of spoiling it. Suddenly words seem all clumsy. Words have got boots on, they could walk all over this lovely feeling I've got. A feeling that's all mine, like Janie's all mine.

Not that she is. All mine, that is. And I nearly said, a moment ago, that finding Janie was finding someone I *belonged* to. But that's not quite right either. Both Clara and Megan keep warning me not to get too excited.

'You must remember,' Clara said, 'that Janie's got a whole life of her own. She's got a husband and a son. And just because you've got fond memories of each other in the past doesn't mean you'll get on now. You'll both have changed. You might not even *like* her, Anna!'

But I knew I would. I knew it as soon as I saw her photograph. Clara brought back lots of photos from her visit to Janie. I look at them every night. There's one of Janie when she was about my age. I stand in front of the mirror with that one, holding it up (even though it's very small) and trying to see the likenesses. There's the snub nose and we've got the same dark, flyaway hair. And I think our legs are the same shape. We've both got nice thin ankles and bumpy knees.

There's other photos too. Photos of Janie with her husband (his name's Bill) and their son Roly. Roly's eight and he looks a bit snooty. I like the look of Bill. He's got one arm round Janie and one hand on Roly's shoulder. But it makes me a bit sad, that photo, because somehow they look like a complete family. Janie works at the Traverse Theatre. I must have looked totally starry-eyed when Clara told me that, but then she said, 'Hold on there, Anna, she's *not* an actress. She works as a cook.' Still, who cares, I thought, she's *in* a theatre. Bill's a printer, though I've no idea what he prints. Clara was vague about it. 'Posters and things,' she said.

Brent was the one I really wanted to talk to about Janie. I thought he'd understand. He was the first person I talked to – really talked to – about my mum. I tried to phone Brent at the Children's Home but whoever I spoke to said Brent couldn't come to the phone. Couldn't? Or wouldn't? He hasn't replied to any of my letters. I thought that maybe writing to him about Janie and joy and all that might not be such a good idea if he was feeling miserable. Sometimes happy people can really get on your nerves. I know. Anyway, I bought him a card with a funny guitar man on the front and I just wrote 'Thinking about you, love Anna' inside, with three kisses. I sent it first class. We still don't know if Brent will have to go to a Children's Hearing or to Court.

I began telling Gemma about Janie, somehow I felt *obliged*. After all, next to Brent, she is my best friend and what's the point of having a best friend if you can't tell her everything? But Gemma's got dozens of aunts and uncles and cousins. She's got a sort of tribe. She doesn't seem to like any of them very much. Moans about having to write thank-you letters after Christmas. How could she understand what it feels like suddenly to find one aunt? So I tried to make it sound very casual.

'My social worker's found an old aunt of mine,' I said.

'Really?' said Gemma, all excited. 'Is she rich and beautiful?'

'Course not,' I said, though actually I was thinking that Janie was more interesting than beautiful. Interesting and a bit exotic.

'She could adopt you,' said Gemma. 'You could live happily ever after.'

That really scared me. I mean even *thinking* happily ever after is enough to make a pig fall on your head.

'Don't be stupid,' I said. 'Janie's married with a son of her own.'

'So . . . ?' said Gemma.

But I couldn't take any more. I dashed off, telling Gemma I was going swimming with Sam, which was true, although not exactly then and there. I thought that maybe when I'd got to know Janie and Janie had got to know me, maybe then I could tell Gemma about her. Perhaps one day I could say, 'My Aunt's invited us both to tea' or, even better still, 'to the theatre'.

I thought I'd meet Janie at her house, but Clara said no, Janie was coming to meet me here at Megan's house and maybe after that, if things went well, I could visit her at her house. So many maybes.

So that's how it happened. Janie came here on Saturday morning. Eleven o'clock and I was awake and washed and dressed by seven. At breakfast, Raymond and Sam were looking really fed up.

Sam said, 'Will my brother come one day, like Anna's aunt?'

Megan said, 'We'll have to see what we can do about that.'

Raymond's been cheerier since his Review, but I bet he was wishing he had an aunt too. Maybe Nerine is a sort of aunt for Raymond.

Megan knows about Nerine now. Apparently she turned up at the Review.

'Was she all dripping wet from the river?' I asked, but Megan said no, that she'd been wearing a wonderful hat.

Megan tried to invite Nerine for tea. Megan does like to make everything and everyone cosy. But somehow I knew in advance that no one could 'cosy' the River Woman. Megan sent Raymond with the invitation but Nerine sent him back with a message written on a brown paper bag in what looked like charcoal. The message was all in capital letters. It said:

> TOO BUSY WITH THE RIVER
> THE RIVER IS TROUBLED
> NEVER GO OUT TO TEA
> RAYMOND IS FRIEND
> PLEASE SEND CAKE

So Megan did. Send a cake, I mean. A big chocolate one covered with Smarties on the top. A cake to drool over. Still, I think Raymond would have liked it if Nerine had come here.

Near eleven o'clock I was so nervous I just couldn't sit down. And I had to keep going to the toilet. I wanted to look out of the window to see her coming, but then I thought that would look just too desperate. Even though desperate was what I was. Desperate for Janie to like me.

Then she was there, wearing a dark blue coat and hat with a long bobble that went down her back like a plait, and she said, 'Anna! At last!' And we hugged. I'd been ready to shake hands. I just didn't want her to know how much I cared. Caring too much puts people off – at least that's how it's been for me in the past. Only hugging seemed natural and Janie seemed as pleased to see me as I was to see her.

Megan made us coffee and let us have the living room

to ourselves. And somehow Janie got me talking. About the last days with Mum, about Jem dying, about the other foster homes I'd been in. Even about Brent and taking the car. And somehow I managed to tell her that *The Wind in the Willows* was my favourite book of all time.

And d'you know, Janie said, 'Well, that's amazing. Roly loves that book, too. I think he's read it about five times.'

Janie told me how much she'd missed Mum and how close they'd been when they were growing up. She'd brought lots more photos. We both cried a bit over the ones of Mum.

'Still,' said Janie, 'now we've found each other.'

'You might disappear like Mum,' I said, because suddenly there was this fear deep down inside me.

Janie put her hands on my shoulder and looked me straight in the eyes.

'Anna, I've no intention of disappearing. Now that you're back in my life, that's where you're staying.'

Then we had another hug and I wondered just how much in her life I was going to stay but I didn't dare ask.

Janie put her coat and hat on again and said, 'You must come and visit me. Meet Bill and Roly. I'll fix it with Clara.'

'That would be nice,' I said. Nice! Understatement of the year!

And suddenly, when Janie had gone, I knew who I could talk to. I ran down to the river. The river was high and burbling to itself. Busy and important. *Her Mighty Majesty the sea*, I thought, *Travelling among the villages incognito.*

There was no one about so I stood under the big willow tree, and I waved my arms about like they were just a couple more branches, and I shouted *'I've found my Aunt Janie! I've found my Aunt Janie!'*

And all the pigeons scooted away as if they'd had the shock of their lives and the river burbled and burbled as if I'd given her one more story to carry. To carry from the past to the future.

Chapter Twenty

NERINE WAS RIGHT about the river being troubled. For days it's been raining as if it was never going to stop. Not just April showers. April *downpours!* You'd go to sleep and it was raining and you'd wake up and it was *still* raining. Windy too. Too windy to keep your umbrella up. And the river's been rising higher and higher – a bit like my excitement about going to visit Janie. I've got two weeks to wait. An eternity!

Anyway, this Thursday, coming home from school with Gemma, the river was lapping at the path. There's some trees growing on very small banks within the river and they were all bent low as if the river was tugging at their roots, wanting to carry them off and away. There was no sign of the swans or the heron. The ducks were all huddled at the edge of the river as if they weren't going to take any chances. Everything was soaked and soggy and by the time I got home, so was I.

The river woke me in the night. It was roaring. I'd never heard it like that before. It was as if it was suddenly angry and trying to tell us so, roaring like that in the middle of the night. By Friday morning there was a Flood Alert. It was on the news and our school was closed! Great! I felt really excited.

'D'you think it will be like the flood in the Bible?' I asked Megan. 'Maybe we should start building an ark.'

'And find two lions, two tigers and two elephants to go in it,' Raymond joked. But I could tell he really fancied an ark because then he said, 'We could make it a small one. Just for us and Toby-dog.'

Actually our house is tall and set high above the river so we're not likely to need an ark or even a boat, but there's lot of houses on streets running at right angles to the river and Megan said it must be very frightening for those people and that there hadn't been a flood for fifty years. Maybe it's our century that the river's angry about.

In the afternoon we all went as far as the bridge to see what was happening. Lots of other people had come to look, too, including the police. There was no sign of Nerine, but I felt sure she was out there somewhere. Maybe doing a Canute act – waving her arms and saying 'Down, river, down!' like we sometimes say to Toby-dog.

Only if she was, she wasn't having much success because now the river had completely covered the path and was still rising. It was almost up to the holes in the wall where the pigeons nest.

If the river was a person, it was like a person who'd suddenly changed character. It made me think of Brent and how you thought you'd got to know him and then he went all moody and glum on you.

The river wasn't like our usual river that mostly drifts along quite gently as if maybe it's humming a little song to itself and is in no great hurry to get anywhere. Sometimes, when the water's low you can see all the different coloured stones on the floor of the river and if you paddled in it, it would just cover over your ankles.

Not now. Now you could see how strong the river was. How all-powerful. How it could sweep everything away. The water was a rich, dark brown. It swept down our stretch and then when it turned a corner to go under the bridge it gathered speed. It was as if it suddenly had a purpose in life. Or had had an urgent message. Get to the sea! Fast! Now!

When it was getting dark we sat at the kitchen table and watched the men from the Council delivering sandbags. They made a kind of wall of them by the bridge, but even as they did it, you knew the river was stronger than that. The rest of the sandbags went to the houses that were built low down, on a level with the river. People stacked them at their gates and doors, each sandbag like a little prayer – 'Please, river, don't come in *my* house.' Earlier in the afternoon Megan took Raymond to check that Nerine was all right but she wasn't in.

I could tell Raymond was worried about her. He wanted to go out and look for her only Megan wouldn't let him.

'Nerine knows the river like no one else does,' she told him. 'She'll be OK.'

'She'll be somewhere safe with the swans and the heron,' I said.

Actually, I was *dying* for the river to flood. I know I shouldn't have been. Partly I thought the river was carrying away all the bad stuff of the past. It was getting ready for the future. Like I was. A future with Janie in it. But also watching the river was like watching a film and waiting for the really dramatic thing to happen and the suspense has you biting your finger nails and wanting to shut your eyes and yet not wanting to miss one second of the film. It was like that. In a way I felt *we* were in a film and this wasn't happening in real life.

Only later, when it really *did* flood, I felt awful about enjoying it all and thinking it was like a film. And that was because of what happened to Sam.

Chapter Twenty-one

I T HAPPENED LIKE THIS. We suddenly discovered that Sam had been nicking things. Lots of things have gone missing lately. Megan's scarf. My pack of Pentels.

One of Brent's CDs (he'd left without it). Raymond's baseball cap and, most recently, his drawing book. Things belonging to everyone – everyone but Sam, that is.

Until it came to Raymond's drawing book, I suppose we all just thought we'd mislaid things. Megan said, 'I must have left my scarf on the bus.' I thought I'd lost my Pentels at school and so on. But Raymond was *frantic* about his drawing book. He said he *knew* he'd left it on his bed. He was absolutely *positive*. And he wanted to draw a picture of the river flooding, so where was it? He made such a fuss that eventually Megan said we'd search the whole house.

And that's how we found it. Raymond's drawing book and everything else we'd 'lost', all in Sam's room.

Sam denied it all. Somehow I think he really *believed* he hadn't stolen anything. Maybe he was just in some kind of a trance when he did it. It's possible. Sometimes your mind just doesn't quite let you know what you're doing. I've heard people say things like 'His left hand doesn't know what his right hand is doing'. So maybe it was like that with Sam. Sam's story went like this:

My Pentels. 'Anna left them in here.'

Megan's scarf. 'I found it in my room one morning.'

Brent's CD. 'No idea how it got here.'

Raymond's baseball cap and drawing book. 'Raymond must have put them under my bed.'

'You *nicked* 'em!' Raymond exploded. But Megan hushed him. Megan said that once, when she was a little girl, her grandma had died and that had made her feel very lonely so she'd stolen a scarf from the school cloakroom because the scarf looked all warm and comfy and she thought it would make her feel better.

'Perhaps,' Megan said, 'you were feeling a bit like that, Sam? I'd like to feel that you could ask for things you wanted instead of stealing them.'

I thought Megan was being really kind and loving and giving Sam a chance to explain and say sorry. But somehow it was the word 'stealing' that seemed to go into Sam like a knife stabbing him.

First he went scarlet. Then his specs steamed up and his mouth went all twisted and funny and he was almost choking on what he wanted to say. And we all stood there waiting and then Sam screamed, 'You stole my mum! You stole her! You stole her!'

And he was gone, out of the house, faster than I've ever seen Sam go before and heading straight for the river. Sam's been such a little zombie lately, I don't know if he was even aware the river was on the point of bursting its banks, breaking down the old wooden bridge as if it was made of matchsticks, bursting through garden walls as if fences, stones and bricks were as easy to knock down as skittles in a bowling alley, and then, before midnight – sweeping right into the nearest houses. The river was letting us know who was boss. The river was doing a take-over. The river was wild as a lion that's just escaped from the zoo.

We all ran after Sam. We didn't even bother to put on coats or wellies – at least Megan grabbed hers but I was in my slippers and Raymond in his trainers. I've no idea where Sam thought he was going. Maybe in that funny little head of his he thought he'd find his mum. Maybe even his brother, Peter. I mean Sam's only eight. And then instead of heading for the road, he slid through a gap in the railings. It's a gap Toby-dog sometimes runs through when he's seen a squirrel or something he wants to chase down on the river bank.

Only there wasn't a bank any more. There was just river, river, river. And Sam being swept away in it like he was no more than a leaf or a branch, part of everything unrooted and uprooted that the river was carrying away to the sea. Somehow Sam's body didn't look like a body any more. Just a dark bundle. He could have been a bag of old rubbish. And he didn't make a sound. I don't suppose he could. Or that even if he did, you wouldn't be able to hear him over the rush and roar of the river.

But you could hear Megan. Megan just stood there screaming, 'Sam! Sam!' Well, it wasn't a scream like I've heard anyone scream before. I used to hear my mum screaming a lot. When she had nothing left to drink. Or when the rent man came and we hadn't any money left. But Megan's scream wasn't like that. Megan's scream was like that of an animal in terrible pain and I thought, How odd! Megan loves him!

And then I wished this *was* a film and not real life. And I thought maybe, in a sort of way, I'd grown to love Sam, too, and if Sam drowned I'd never forgive myself for all the nasty things I'd said to him and for washing Erasmus like that when Sam liked him much better all smelly. Or for telling him not to stuff his face when I suppose Sam wasn't just hungry for food, he was hungry for *love*. And I wished I could scream like Megan because I could feel a scream in my chest and in my throat only nothing would come out. Nothing at all.

Then just when I thought there was no hope, no hope at all, the river swept Sam into the almost submerged trunk of a willow tree and jammed him there. At least either the river swept him there or the willow tree caught him, like you see a dad catching a runaway toddler. And the next minute there was a figure dragging Sam out like he was a small wet sandbag. A figure in wellies and a long mac.

'Nerine!' we all said at once. Megan had her hands over her face as if she was praying and I think we were all crying. I know I was. Nerine climbed up over what remained of the bank until she was on dry ground. She laid Sam on his side and thumped him on the back until he coughed up at least a gallon of river.

We were all round him by then, Megan weeping over him and Raymond and I taking off our jerseys to wrap round him.

Before we had time to thank Nerine, she'd gone.

'Trouble over,' I heard her say.

Sam opened his eyes and said, 'Only borrowed things.'

'Of course you did, darling,' Megan said. Then we carried him home and he had a hot bath and we all had hot chocolate only Sam fell asleep over his and hardly woke up when Megan undressed him and put him to bed.

The river roared all night and our house seemed to rock in the wind. It felt a bit as if we *were* in an ark.

I lay there listening to the river and the wind and thought how Megan, Raymond, Sam and I had almost become a family without thinking about it. That maybe being a family was something that crept up on you. And then I thought about Janie. At least I thought about how hard I tried *not* to think about Janie. About the possibility I might go and live with her for ever and ever, that she might adopt me.

I know she can't. Not without my mum agreeing and as no one knows where she is, there's no chance of that. Clara says that Janie could get 'parental rights and responsibilities' which would mean that she'd be like a parent and I could live with her for ever, but that I shouldn't think of it. Building my hopes up like that could lead to awful disappointment. Only it was impossible *not* to think of it.

But lying there, snug under my duvet, hearing Raymond mumbling in his sleep next door and Megan's familiar footsteps on the stairs and knowing Sam was cuddled up safe with Erasmus, I thought, did I really want to leave here and go and live with Janie? And I didn't know any more.

Chapter Twenty-two

EVERYONE's been fussing over Sam. And Sam's been lapping it up! The doctor came and listened to his chest and looked down his throat and in his ears and said, 'I think he'll live. He's quite a tough wee chap.' Sam looked very proud of himself.

He lost his specs in the river so Megan had to take his prescription to the optician and get him a new pair. He stayed in bed all weekend and Raymond and I took it in turns to play with him. Megan was up and down bringing him drinks and fruit and comics and puzzle books. Even Toby-dog took to sitting on his bed and Megan just said, 'Ah well,' and let him!

Sitting up in bed, all smiley, Sam looked like a different boy. It was a bit as if the river had washed all his old hurts away. That zombie look had vanished and it wasn't just the new specs. It was somehow as if Sam was inside himself again and before he'd been – well – missing.

I've been thinking that my first idea about Nerine might have been right and that she is a kind of river nymph in disguise and that like Pan, in *The Wind in the Willows*, she's here to look after Nature, or at least our river. And then I know that can't really be true and that Nerine's just an ordinary old woman, who's nuts on the river. But that's not quite right either. I think she's both. Ordinary and Magical. I think we all are.

Anyway, of course we all wanted to thank Nerine but we didn't know how.

'She's just not very keen on people,' said Megan.

'She probably rescued Sam because he was making the river untidy,' I joked.

'Of course that wasn't it,' said Raymond crossly. 'She's very kind. And shy.'

'And she just likes *you*,' said Megan.

'Because I like the river,' said Raymond.

'What about a thank-you present?' asked Megan.

'She'd like some new wellies,' said Raymond. 'Those big long waders would be good – and maybe a woolly hat.'

'And flowers,' said Megan. 'A big bunch of flowers.'

'I'm not sure she's a flowery person,' said Raymond.

'Everyone's a flowery person,' said Megan.

So Megan bought Nerine a pair of waders (Raymond found out the size) and I helped choose a really warm woolly hat. It was red and orange and had flaps to come over Nerine's ears and a kind of bobbly tail at the top. It was very jolly.

And we all did her a card. Raymond did the picture on the front. It was a really dramatic picture of the river and Sam in it with a little balloon coming out of his head saying 'Help! Help!'

Sam did a border all round the picture. It was a pattern of zig-zags and crosses in all different colours. I let him use my Pentels. Inside Sam wrote 'THANK YOU FOR SAVING MY LIFE, LOVE SAM'. And I did a verse! I'm getting good at these. This one was:

> By the river's the place to be,
> The river that runs away to the sea.
> Sometimes the river's angry and wild
> But mostly the river's gentle and mild
> Keep the river clean and clear
> Because, to us, the river's dear.

It took me ages that one. Megan found some lines from a poet called Gerard Manley Hopkins. I have to admit his poem was quite a lot better than mine, so I copied it out on the back of the card. It went like this:

> What would the world be, once bereft
> Of wet and wildness? Let them be left,
> O let them be left, wildness and wet;
> Long live the weeds and the wilderness yet.

I think Nerine was very pleased with her waders and her hat and our card because she sent us another message (via Raymond, of course) and written on another brown paper bag. I think I might start using paper bags myself. There's something rather stylish about them and anyway, it's recycling paper, isn't it?

Nerine's paper bag said:

I LIKE MY HAT. I LIKE MY WADERS.
I LIKE THE FLOWERS AND CARD MOST.
NERINE

'There you are,' said Megan. 'I told you she'd like the flowers.'

Actually I think the best present we could give to Nerine was the weekend we spent after the flood and when Sam was up and out of bed – a weekend cleaning up the river.

You've never seen such a mess as there was after the flood. It made you realise how careless everyone is because almost every branch of every bush and tree was draped with bits of plastic. There were carrier bags and black bin liners and sacks and every sort of rubbish you can imagine. It looked as if the river was having a very odd kind of jumble sale and had hung everything up for people to see and buy.

Reeds and leaves and twigs and broken branches had all got tangled together so that it looked as if the river had spent the night knitting or making patchwork quilts in greens and browns. Maybe, I thought, that's what the river had been angry about – all the junk thrown in it. So it had decided to rush and roar and throw everything out. After all, it was April. Time for spring cleaning.

It took the best part of Saturday and Sunday to gather all the junk up into bin bags. Lots of people helped. They brought shears and secateurs and rakes. It was fun getting really muddy and wet and trying to reach a bit of plastic that was almost but not quite out of your reach. Megan made us all wear gloves and wellies, but we still got very wet. Nerine kept away. Too many people, I suppose, but I bet she'll be pleased and there's loads of stuff to make into a terrific bonfire. All sorts of odd things were found that the river had abandoned in its rush to the sea – chair legs, road signs and suitcases. I read in the local paper afterwards that someone had found a black pudding!

And then on Monday Sam had the best piece of news ever. His mum has had the new baby and he's going home! And no, I don't feel jealous because next Sunday I'm going to visit Janie! It's just a visit, I keep telling myself. Just a visit.

Chapter Twenty-three

I couldn't help it. Walking into Janie's flat that Sunday morning, the questions just took over my mind. Could I live here? Could I feel at home here? How many bedrooms are there? Is there room for me?

Of course I didn't ask any of them out loud. I was just worried that they showed in my eyes. I'd had a terrible time getting dressed for the visit. I've got two skirts and one dress. I tried the skirts on with every jersey I've got (six). I even considered my school uniform! In the end I settled for jeans and the velvety top Megan bought me. It was a half-and-half decision. Half casual and half special occasion. I remembered that Janie had quite an exotic look so at the last moment I pinned a red poppy in my hair. I'd found it in one of the charity shops. I think it came off a hat. I'd washed my hair and scrubbed my nails. I'd even clipped my toenails. I think I had some mad idea that Janie might suggest dancing barefoot.

Clara took me to the flat, though she didn't stay. It was on the top floor of a tenement block. I remember Brent telling me that tenements used to be for the poor but now they were up-market and trendy. It was certainly up! Up so many stairs I thought I'd be all sweaty by the time we got there. The door was already open in a welcoming sort of way so all Clara had to do was poke her head in and call, 'Helloooh! We're here!' And there was Janie, still in her dressing gown and with a piece of toast in her hand.

I didn't have to say anything because Janie was so chatty. I was glad. Janie's chattiness gave me time to catch my breath and stop shaking.

'We've all had a lie-in this morning. Could you go for a second breakfast? Bill's doing toast. It's about the only thing he can cook. If you call making toast cooking, which

I don't. Let's hang your coat up. Clara? Would you like coffee? Goodness knows where Roly's got to, we'll find him in a minute. Come in, come in, come in!'

Because it was on the top floor, Janie's flat was made up of attics. Not a flat ceiling anywhere and windows that looked out on chimney pots. In a room off the hall where Janie was hanging up my coat, I saw a small figure hunched over a computer.

'Roly, say hello to Anna,' called Janie.

There was a grunt from the figure at the computer which could have been 'hello' but might have been 'get lost!'

Before I knew it, there I was, in Janie's sitting room, with Clara calling goodbye and me trying to take everything in – the shelves and shelves of books, the potted plants everywhere so that it wouldn't have surprised me if the chimneys outside started sprouting them, and a table with Bill at it eating toast and the Sunday papers.

'You look after Anna while I get dressed,' Janie told Bill.

'Umm. I will if she tells me if she likes marmalade, honey or jam on her toast,' said Bill.

I liked the look of Bill. He didn't get up and start shaking my hand or anything awful like that. He was short, broad shouldered and more or less bald. There was a kind of monkish fringe round the outside of his head. But he had sea-blue eyes and a big smile. Did my dad look like Bill? I wondered. Then I told myself to 'cut', cut it out. I'd decided there were useful questions to ask yourself and questions that got you absolutely nowhere. Wondering about my dad was one of them.

'Like the poppy,' Bill said, looking at my hair. 'Janie's got a sunflower she sometimes sticks in her hat. Roly!' he shouted. 'Get yourself in here!'

There was a slightly louder grunt from the room off the hall.

'Boys!' said Bill, handing me a plate of toast. 'That one's computer mad. I'd have you know, we're not a particularly dysfunctional family. Do you know any completely functional ones?'

'No,' I said. 'No, I don't.'

Actually I didn't much feel like toast, but it seemed rude not to eat any, so I managed a piece and a half before Janie came back.

Janie showed me round the flat. The kitchen was tiny. It could have been a ship's galley and us up high, sailing over the city. Roly had firmly closed his door by now and hung a *Danger: Radiation* sign on it.

'Charming!' said Janie. 'We'll catch up with him later.'

Janie and Bill's bedroom was mostly bed with a lot of clothes strewn about and books flung down on the floor. Bill had a study. It was lovely and messy with a drawing board and jars of pens and posters and book jackets stuck on the walls as if Bill was making a new kind of wallpaper, improvising as he went along.

'That's what Bill does,' said Janie. 'Designs book jackets and posters.' I thought of the poster I'd seen in the police station, the one of the handcuffed hands and the words DEALT WITH and hoped Bill hadn't done that one.

And then there was another bedroom. An empty bedroom with just a small divan bed in it, a chest of drawers and a mirror. The ceiling sloped, of course, and the window was like half a window, just squeezed in under the roof.

'If you stand on the bed you can get a glimpse of the sea,' said Janie. So I did. And I could. Just a glimpse of the sea and the docks and a few seagulls keeping watch.

Was Janie thinking what I was thinking? This could be my room? I don't know. Neither of us said anything. There was just an awkward kind of silence, then we both smiled at each other and Janie said, 'I thought you might like to see the theatre this afternoon.' Would I!

So that's what we did after lunch. Lunch was soup and cheese and there was still no sign of Roly. He must have sneaked into the kitchen and helped himself to something. I began to really dislike Roly even without meeting him. I had to remind myself that Janie had told me that he loved *The Wind in the Willows* so he couldn't be entirely awful. Unless he was like one of the weasels in the book, that is.

I forgot about Roly when we went down to The Traverse Theatre. It's really two theatres, a big comfy one and a small uncomfy one. Both of them are very plain with black walls as if whatever they're doing there is very serious and not just entertainment. Janie says they put on plays by all the new writers there. *Avant garde* she called it. I thought maybe I could try writing a play instead of stories and poems though if I wanted to write about people like Raymond and Nerine and Roly I'd have to invent a lot of dialogue.

The bar and restaurant where Janie works is down in the basement. Dim lights and iron pillars covered in posters and one of those sleek, silvery bar counters which you'd like to stroke, and stools to perch on and people not much older than me only with amazing hair cuts serving behind the bar. It was all very, very trendy. Brent would love this, I thought, and got a sudden pang, wishing he'd answer my letters, wishing I could bring him here, wishing I could tell him all about Janie and Bill and the invisible Roly.

After that we went back to the flat and had tea and more toast. (I began to wonder if Janie and Bill lived on toast. Maybe being a cook at the theatre means Janie doesn't do any cooking at home.) Roly had gone out to a friend's house.

'You'll meet him next time,' Janie said. And Bill drove me back to Megan's. He parked outside and sat there stroking his bald head as if struggling to say something. I was just about to get out when he said, 'Don't worry about Roly. He's just a bit bothered because Janie's always wanted a daughter.' Then he gave me a little peck on the cheek. I tell you, I went in *singing*.

Trust Clara to bring me down to earth.

'Well, you *can't* be her daughter!' Clara said crisply. 'You're her niece. Let that be enough for you, Anna.'

Actually, I hardly needed Clara to bring me down to earth. Other people's parents were doing that. Sam's mother for a start. You'd think she'd be really pleased to see him, wouldn't you? Particularly as there nearly *wasn't* a Sam.

The first thing she says to him is, 'What d'you mean by going and nearly drowning yourself? You never did look where you was going, did he, Peter?'

Because yes, Sam's brother Peter is home too. Got fed up living with his dad apparently and hitch-hiked back from London.

Peter said, 'Yes, two left feet, our Sam,' but he said it all friendly and with a big smile and you could tell he was really pleased to see Sam again.

'And you,' Sam's mum said to Megan, 'call yourself a carer?'

'It wasn't her fault,' I said. But I just got a dirty look. She had the new baby with her. It was a little girl. Peter held her mostly and she was all pale and pukey and to judge from the smell, I think she needed a new nappy.

'What d'you think of your new sister then?' Sam's mum asked.

'Very nice,' said Sam.

'You'll have to behave yourself now,' said his mum. 'When we get home. I've got enough on my plate with this new one without you creating havoc and getting into trouble. Got your things now?'

'I've packed them for him,' said Megan.

'Least you could do,' said Sam's mum – not one bit grateful.

So off they went, and Sam so happy he only just remembered to give Megan a hug and say goodbye to Raymond and me.

Megan and I watched them going down the road, Sam trailing a bit because he's still got a limp and his mum turning round and shouting 'Hurry up, can't you. I haven't got all day. Got to feed the babba. And I suppose you'll be wanting something to eat.'

'You can't kiss it better,' Megan said, out of the blue.

'Kiss *what* better?' I asked.

'Oh nothing,' said Megan. 'It's just something Raymond said.'

Sometimes I think that although Megan tries hard to love us all equally, Raymond's her favourite.

Anyway, the amazing thing is, Sam didn't seem to mind his mum moaning and shouting at him. I think if she'd beaten him over the head he'd still have looked happy. And I wouldn't put it past her to do just that as soon as she got him round the corner, out of sight. I was glad Peter was there and I saw him put his arm round Sam. What I think is this. Kids are nice. Kids know how to love. Grown-ups forget.

Megan just gave this huge sigh and said, 'I hope it works out for him. I hope she looks after him.'

It was only a day after Sam had left that we had another Awful Parent. Guess who? Brent's dad. Brent's dad storming in, saying, 'Is he here? Where is he?'

'I beg your pardon . . .' said Megan.

Brent's dad didn't take a blind bit of notice. He looked really wild-eyed and desperate and he went charging up the stairs, looking in every room.

'Mr Windward,' said Megan. 'Please calm down. If it's Brent you're looking for, I can assure you he's not here.'

He did calm down a bit then and Megan took him into the kitchen and made him a cup of tea. I peeped in just once and could hardly believe my eyes. All the anger had gone out of Brent's dad. He was limp as a popped balloon. And crying. Sobbing really so that he used up almost the whole box of Megan's tissues.

It seems Brent's run away from the children's home and no one knows where he is. They think he's on the streets. Brent's dad said he'd searched the city without finding him and now he was going to look in Glasgow and then London. But he could be anywhere. I almost felt sorry for him. Almost.

I felt sorrier for Brent. I suppose he was scared he'd

have to go to court, though only a few days later Megan told me it was going to be a Children's Hearing and probably there'd just be a Warning from the Police Inspector and Brent would be sent to another foster home.

In bed that night I thought of the people I'd seen living on the street and some of them as young as Brent. They sit there even when it's freezing cold. Some of them have an old blanket or maybe a dog, though I don't think Brent will have a dog. And sometimes they have a bit of cardboard saying *Homeless and hungry*. It made me cry to think of Brent living like that.

I thought of the card I'd given him and the poem inside –

> Wherever you are
> Near or far
> Wherever you go
> I want you to know
> I'll be your friend
> Time without end

Only when I wrote that I hadn't been thinking that Brent would really be far away or that I wouldn't know where he was. I'd be thinking that one day, when I was older and earning lots of money, we'd all live together, Brent, Raymond and me.

But that was before Janie. And before *the really amazing news!*

Janie and Bill have applied for Parental Rights and Responsibilities. I keep going over and over that phrase because it sounds so grim.

'It sounds,' said Bill, 'as if being a parent is like having to carry heavy sacks of coal for the rest of your life.'

And Roly said – because yes, I've actually met Roly and we've talked together and, surprise, surprise, I think we *quite* like each other – 'When actually your lives would be dead boring without us!'

So! So I'm being *uplifted*! Into a family. My own family.

But wherever I am, I'll still be Brent's friend 'time without end'. And Raymond's. And Sam's. And Megan's.

Postscript

5 CLAREMONT PARK, LEITH, EDINBURGH EH6

14th June, 2002

Dear favourite foster Mum!

I'm still settling in. I know you told me it would take a while and you were right. I wake up in the morning wondering where I am and missing you and my room and Toby-dog and Raymond – oh and the river. Then I stand on my bed and look beyond the chimney pots to the sea. *Her Mighty Majesty the sea*, like that poem says, and I remind myself that the river is part of it.

Isn't it odd how a different house has different sounds? The radiators here don't gurgle like yours do and even the sound of the front door closing is different and at night I hear traffic instead of river.

Please keep sending me postcards because although I'm really happy to be here, everything still feels a bit strange – like I keep forgetting where the teaspoons are and where the towels are kept.

I know Janie's my aunt and I know I'm *family*, but it doesn't quite feel like a family yet. We're all still getting to know each other. Last night Bill asked me how long I thought it took to get to know someone. I said I thought about six months. Bill laughed. He said, 'I've known Janie for seventeen years and there are still things I don't know about her. She still surprises me. I like that.'

I liked that, too. I thought it meant we weren't in a hurry to get to know each other. We could take our time. Perhaps that's what being part of a family means – having lots of time to get to know each other. And being surprised!

Roly is a surprise, by the way. He's been quite nice to

me! And yesterday he actually let me use his computer and showed me how to send e-mails. We've had a few rows though. Mainly about TV programmes – he likes the most *boring* programmes – and who has the bathroom first. And he got cross because Janie lets me stay up an hour longer than him, which is only fair because I *am* older. But Roly doesn't think it's fair. We are agreed that *The Wind in the Willows* is the best book ever, though Roly likes Ratty best and I like Mole.

Janie keeps asking me I'm all right and if I'm happy and I wish she'd stop because I can hardly say no, I'm not all right, can I? And sometimes I *don't* feel all right. I feel all wrong, as if half of me is still at 21 Teviotdale Place and the other half is here and somehow I haven't quite joined up the old Anna and the new Anna. I don't like to tell Janie this because I think it would upset her and I can tell she really wants me to feel at home.

We've done lots of things together though, like going to the hairdresser's (a really posh one) and shopping and last Sunday we all went for a walk round the docks and then went for a pizza and it looked as if every family in Edinburgh was doing just the same. Janie says that in the holidays she'll try and find me some work at the theatre. Bill and I collected Janie from the theatre last night and the man in the box office asked if I was her daughter. Janie went quite red. I could tell she was really pleased. (And so was I!) Anyway, she just said, 'No, this is my niece.'

Are your new children – Tracy and Mike – feeling at home? Which of them has my room? Sometimes I picture one of them in *my* bed and it feels very odd. Anyway, I'll meet them when I come on a visit. And I'll see Raymond and Sam again. Fancy Sam coming back to you so soon! I used to hate moving from place to place. I remember once going back to my mum and it lasted about three weeks. It was horrible. So I know how Sam must be feeling.

Janie comes and tucks me in every night as if I was about five. But actually I like it! She says she was very lucky to find me. But I think I'm the lucky one really.

All the same, I miss you
Lots and lots of love,
Anna xxxxxxxxxx

Dear Raymond,

Thank you very much for the picture of the heron. I've put it on my bedroom wall. Janie says I can stick up as many pictures as I like so please send me some more. I like the way you've drawn the heron standing on one leg. I've tried standing on one leg myself and it's not at all easy.

How are you getting on with Tracy and Mike? Course I know they can't be as wonderful as me!!!

I told Janie and Bill about you and the river and they said that when you come on a visit we'll show you the docks and maybe you can draw some pictures of the boats.

Give Sam a big hug from me, will you, and tell him that Janie is showing me how to knit so I'm going to knit a scarf for Erasmus.

I miss Toby-dog. The man in the flat below has a cat called Toggle. He's ginger and rather snooty.

I miss you too.

lots of love from your very own foster-sis.

Anna xxx

P.S. Hope you won't mind a paper kiss or three!

From: Anna Charlston <j.hamilton@gateway.com>
To: <gemma.ford@virgin.net>
Sent: 19 June 2002 20.18

Hi Gemma!

Roly's allowed me all of 10 mins to send you this! Janie says would you like to come 2 the theatre with us nxt Sat nt? It's a play called *My Magic Football Hat*! (*Wow! I can do italic!*) Janie says you can stay over too. C U tomorrow.

love, Anna xx

19 June, 2002

Dear Brent,

When I go and visit Megan, I'm going to put this letter in a bottle and 'post' it in the river. I don't suppose Raymond and Nerine would approve, but I don't think the river will mind too much. And one day this letter might reach you.

I think about you a lot and wish you hadn't run away because I think you must be feeling very sad and lonely. And if you are living on the streets it must get very cold.

I remember you saying 'Who cares' over and over again. So this is to say, I DO. Sometimes I think that just one person caring out of a whole big world of people who don't care isn't very much. And then I think that just one person caring can make a world of difference.

So wherever you are in the world, Brent, I'll be sending you love. It'll be flying through the air and floating down the river towards you. I wish that on a cold night it could warm you.

your friend for always,
Anna xxx